LITTLE WORKHOUSE EMILY

DOLLY PRICE

PUREREAD.COM

CONTENTS

DEAR READER, GET READY FOR ANOTHER GREAT STORY...

A VICTORIAN ROMANCE

Turn the page and let's begin

MARY LUCAS

Mary Lucas, a parlourmaid of seventeen, had the good luck (or so she thought at the time) of attracting the notice of a young man who was her superior in society, the nephew of her mistress, Mrs Althea Loft. Frederick Collins was twenty-five and should have known better than to flirt with the young girl with the wide blue eyes and chestnut curls that peeked from under her maid's cap, but how was he to know that Mary Lucas thrived on romantic novels in which dashing men of means fell in love with, and married servants and seamstresses and milliners? Poor Mary Lucas was an avid reader of such fiction, but while she knew the stories were the fruit of someone's imagination and hurried pen, she chose to believe them, and longed for this to happen to her.

Frederick stayed a summer with his widowed aunt at the house in Cotham, Bristol. He was a young man without principle, intent only on enjoying himself. Mary was easily taken in, he flattered her and told her he loved her, and they met in the woods and in the apartment of an obliging friend who made himself absent on Mary's afternoon off.

Mary was in no doubt as to his sincerity. It was incomprehensible to her that anybody should say they were in love if love was not there. He took full advantage of her devotion to him. Mary wavered at first – it was a sin, and the girls in the books never succumbed before marriage – but he said he loved her, and he was very much in need of her, he said, and apt to *suffer greatly* if she did not give herself to him. So she gave in to spare him suffering.

He got Mary with child and she was sure in late August. She was thrilled, delighted – marriage would happen before winter! Frederick was to go away in a few days, and it was good this happened before he left, for she wouldn't have to tell him in a letter; she could tell him face to face and see his eyes light up. She dreamed of a sweet little house in Clifton or Westbury or Abbots Leigh. She planned the wallpaper and the curtains and wrote to her mother in Devon that she was getting married and please could she send on the white linen lace-edged sheets promised to her upon her marriage.

"We're going to be so 'appy you an' me," she said dreamily to Frederick, when they next met. It was to be their last meeting before he had to return to Oxford. They were lying by a pretty stream that gurgled over stones and rocks and were hidden from view by a row of trees in full leaf. They had been there for an hour or more, and her heart tingled at the thought of telling him their news. The gurgling water rang in her ears like wedding chimes.

"What is that, Bluebell?" He called her Bluebell because of her eyes.

"We're going to be so 'appy, you an' me both. An' – the baby," she added coyly.

"The baby," he said, and it seemed to Mary that he was surprised. He sat up suddenly, brushing her off. "What baby?"

"Our baby, Freddie! Isn't it wonderful?"

"Are you sure?"

"Yes, I went to the doctor because I was feelin' very poorly an' he told me, and he asked me was I gettin' married and I said yes of course I was gettin' married, I'm not the sort of girl to lie wiv a man without luv an' marriage in the picture. He said better do it soon Miss, because it will soon be obvious to everybody an' you wouldn't want to walk down the aisle with everyone knowin'."

Frederick was silent.

"I never thought of marriage, Bluebell," he said at last.

"Oh, but if we luv each other, marriage follows don't it," Mary said with confidence. "An' we luv each other."

"Marriage – that's a different prospect. You see, I – I can't marry you, Bluebell."

"You can't? Why not?"

"Don't look so astonished, Mary. Surely you knew that marriage between us would be impossible." He muttered under his breath.

"Why are you cursin', Freddie?"

"Because you do not understand. Have you not noticed there is a wide gap between my world and yours?"

"Yes, but – that don't matter when we luv each other."

"Of course it matters. I can't marry you, Mary. I'm sorry if I gave you some wrong impression, but I never promised you marriage. Never mentioned the word marriage. I didn't for one moment think you expected it. My life would be over if I married – you. You have no fortune or – or connections, you know, that sort of thing."

The lack of fortunes were never a concern to the dashing heroes in Mary's books. Where there was love, money did not matter one whit.

"Money don't matter, Freddie."

He looked at her as if they had only just met.

"You can't possibly be so stupid," he said. He got up from the grass and took his hat. "Good day to you, Mary Lucas."

"Frederick!" she called after him. She smoothed down her gown and brushed off the leaves and grasses and hurried after him. But he had disappeared. She made her way back to the house as quickly as she could, but he was not there. He was present for dinner but did not look her way once. He left early the following morning and Mary hoped for some days that he would return. She waited for a letter, but the only letter was from her mother congratulating her and saying that she would send on the sheets which had been carefully preserved in camphor.

FREDERICK'S AUNT
ALTHEA LOFT

Mrs Loft's house was a small establishment with a cook, a maid and a man. She had been married to a ship's captain who had been lost at sea and had no children of her own. She was not house-proud and her home still had faded wallpaper from the first residents in the 1700's. It was full of artifacts and souvenirs of her husband's voyages. She burned candles sparingly. The overall impression to a visitor was that it was a shoddy, cluttered, dark house.

When a large parcel arrived for Mary, Mrs Loft was curious about it and in a light-hearted way asked her what it contained as she dusted the parlour one morning.

Mary thought she had nothing to lose by telling her.

"It's my mother's best sheets, Ma'am. A wedding gift to 'er from 'er mistress, it was. It was put away for me. You see, I

– I'm supposed to be gettin' married. Did – did he tell you?"

"Who? Who tell me? Who?"

"Your nephew Frederick, Ma'am."

"What about Mr Frederick? What has it to do with him?"

"We're sweethearts, Ma'am."

"Do not be utterly ridiculous. What has gotten into your head? Are you completely mad? Frederick! Mr Frederick to you!"

Mary became bolder. If Frederick wasn't willing to marry her, perhaps his aunt could make him, out of common decency.

"I'm expectin' his child, Ma'am, I am."

All hell broke loose in the house. Mrs Anderson the cook and Michael the man, busy downstairs, stopped their jobs and listened to the din coming from the parlour where Mary had been quietly dusting. Whatever had she done? Broken the vase the late Captain had brought back from China? They came up the passage from where they could see the front hallway with the sunlight slanting in through the stained glass transom of the front door, making a beam that rested on the floor. They heard a door open and suddenly Mary appeared in the hall, caught by the sunbeam, crying bitterly, followed by Mrs Loft in a great temper, a rage they had never beheld before.

"Get out! You tramp! You liar! You shall not stay another minute in this house! Get your miserable belongings together and get out! Liar!" The two servants withdrew hurriedly lest they were seen and gaped at each other. Mick was amazed but Mrs Anderson nodded and sighed knowingly.

"I thought so, I did," she said. Mick shook his head and Mrs Anderson had to explain that she had seen Mary's girth expand of late.

"An I know who it is too," she said, going back to stir the soup. "Aye, I know well who it is. But I can't say a word!"

"I can guess that for myself," was Mick's reply. "He won't marry 'er."

"Poor stupid girl," said Mrs Anderson. "She wasn't the first, and she won't be the last that gave in to a scoundrel. Her life is ruined."

Mary went home to Devon, taking the linen sheets back with her. She held the parcel in front of her as she made her way through the muddy village to hide her condition. But there was no hiding it from her mother and father, and no compassion, no sympathy for her either – she was to go straight back to Bristol on the first train in the morning in case any of the neighbours saw her like that and she was to tell her mistress that she insisted on some recompense. They'd never live it down.

They wanted nothing to do with her. Mary returned to Bristol, was refused entry at the Cotham house and ended up in Yellowhill Workhouse. The following March she gave birth to a healthy girl she named Emily after Frederick's older sister whom she had never met. She still believed that someday he would return repentant and marry her. Poor Mary Lucas would continue to believe in love until her dying day, and that was only five short years off.

"I DON'T LIKE PEOPLE"

F our years went by. Emily was a sturdy little girl and not knowing any world outside the thick grey walls, was content. She did not see any children with colourful or stylish clothes, so her uniform of washed out blue with its pinny the colour of porridge seemed perfectly normal to her. Her little friends wore the same. She did not have a papa, and neither did Lynn, Anne, Joe or Jenny. So that was normal too. She had a mama though, and some of her little friends did not, so she considered herself better off than they. Her mama worked in the kitchen and she was allowed to be with her as long as she sat in a corner out of the way.

"She's very quiet and well-behaved," remarked Mrs Kealy as they peeled potatoes one day.

"She's too quiet," her mother said. "She thinks this is her 'ome and knows nothink about the world out there. I'm goin' to take her away soon. I'll get a job, and she'll have a normal life playin' with other children on the road and I'll get her a puppy. I grew up in the country. This place is no life for a child."

"What will you do, Mary?"

"I don't know yet, but I'm going before she turns five."

In early spring, Mary had an opportunity to leave. Another inmate Mrs Porter had been offered a situation and the employer needed another hand. They would have a room in a large tenement. It was like a dream come true, not her most cherished dream, but if she could leave here then, anything was possible. Emily caught her enthusiasm. Mary was given her own clothes back, and a set of hand-me-down clothes for Emily whose little owner had died.

Emily loved her clothes and the two set happily out of the gate. But that was the end of Emily's happiness. As the large building was left farther and farther behind, she grew fretful and squeezed her mother's hand tightly.

They walked along a busy street and she clung to her mother's skirts.

"I don't like people," she said, eyeing the multitudes hurrying past.

"Oh don't be silly, Emily. The world is full of people! They're just like the people in the workhouse."

"I don't like men," Emily whispered, as a trio of businessmen with beards and top hats passed by. "They're big and ugly with whiskers."

"Oh stop yer nonsense! They won't do you any 'arm! There'll come a day when you'll like them well enough! Now look at that lady with the pretty parasol."

"I don't like 'er," Emily was determined to hate everything about the world outside the workhouse. "I don't know 'er."

They went down a side street, then into a small court with large run-down buildings, full of washing hanging out the windows and people shouting to each other.

"You must be nice here and play with the other children," Mary told her as they passed a noisy group of boys and girls jumping and skipping.

"I don't like 'em. I only like the children I know."

Emily did not like the room either. It smelled different than the workhouse. The only bright prospect was that she did not have to share her mother with anybody except Mrs Porter. But the first morning, when she woke, her mother and Mrs Porter were gone and she began to wail.

A bigger girl appeared in the doorway.

"Come on upstairs, you're to spend the day with us. Come on, stop cryin'! Cry baby!"

The girl was in charge of several smaller children and ruled them with a rod of iron. Her name was Hetty, she was twelve years old.

Emily did not like her either.

"Where's Mama?" she asked her.

"She's out workin' at the Ferrells Factory. An' my mother too an' Mrs Porter. Eat your bread."

It was stale, different from the workhouse bread.

"I don't like it."

"Go hungry then!"

Emily nibbled the bread.

But just as Emily was getting used to the different bread, different soup and people everywhere, big men with beards and snorting horses, everything changed again. Mrs Porter changed her mind about Mary Lucas. She was not good at the machines and talked too much, getting her into trouble, making her look bad opposite the foreman. Mrs Porter let it drop one day that Mary Lucas had a child outside wedlock, and that was that. She was dismissed, and she and Emily went back to the workhouse.

SADNESS

A great deal of change had taken place in Yellowhill since they had last been there.

The old Master had retired, and a new man installed, together with his wife, who was to be Matron.

The workings of how the Union was staffed was quite unknown to Mary Lucas and to most of the other inmates, and little did she care. But there were always a few seasoned women who by some astonishing detection of their own, knew exactly what was going on in the upper echelons, the Boardroom in the handsome building fronting the street where the Guardians met to discuss how best to solve 'the pauper problem'. It was Mrs Simpson who reported that the new Master had a cousin a *member*, and that was how he got the posting, fer she knew, for a fact, that he himself was a wicked greedy man.

"What's a member?" Mary asked.

"Lawks, you're ignorant. A member of Parliament!"

"But shouldn't that do us good then?"

"That's what the Guv'nor said. That Mr Coates 'aving a member for a relation would bring in improvements and favours, but the vicar, Mr Somerset, bless his heart, said that Mr Coates character was most important to him, regardless of who 'e was related to, and the others shouted the vicar down, and said of course 'e was of an excellent character and nobody could be found of better, so the vicar spoke no more."

"Maybe he is of good character, then." Mary said hopefully.

"Mary, you're innocent. Tha's why you're 'ere. At least you've given up 'oping that rascal will claim you and Em'ly. Haven't you? He's married by now, I bet."

Mary did not reply. She still sometimes hoped that a conversion of heart would bring Frederick looking for her. He would take her and Emily away from this place in a carriage pulled by four handsome horses, and vow to make good his neglect and cruelty for the rest of his life. But the feeling was not as strong as before; there were few if any books in the workhouse and certainly no novels, and nothing to feed her hopes. They were dwindling with every passing month.

As for his aunt! Now there was a cruel woman indeed. Mary had never returned there except to get two weeks wages she had been entitled to.

Emily's little sojourn in the world had educated her in some ways.

"Mama, why don't some people have papas?"

"Some peoples' papas are dead, or they 'ave to be away workin'."

"Do I have a papa?"

There it was, the dreaded question.

"No, not for a long time now."

"But I did have? Once?"

"Yes, once."

"Where is he now?"

"He 'ad to go away. Some papas go away."

"Will he ever come back then?"

Mary hated answering this question, for it meant she would have to choose between her own dreams and reality. She struggled for a moment.

"No, he won't," she said with regret. She felt a sort of numbing sadness, the kind that doesn't produce tears but weighs upon the heart.

"I don't mind," Emily said. "Are we going to stay 'ere now, Mama?"

"No, we're only 'ere for a short time more." Mary was determined not to allow Emily to grow up there. She had to know the world. Perhaps she, Mary, could find another chance to work outside and even marry. This time, she would be very careful to get the ring on her finger before giving herself to a man.

Emily was not pleased to hear they were going to leave the workhouse again.

"I don't know what's amiss with that child," her mother sighed to her friend Janey, who had also been a servant whose sweetheart, another servant, had deserted her when she had got with child. "Why don't she like people?"

"I'll tell you why she don't like people, Mary. When we were in the nursery, you an' me it was, and nobody visited except to berate us for being poor and simple. The Matron scolded you for falling by th'wayside, an' me too. Dr 'Orrocks was 'orrid too cos we was not married women. We was there fir three years and the only people we saw was those, an' then there was the tour of the Guv'nors every now and then, and they standin' there just lookin' down their noses at us and asking questions, and no kindness, they goin' away again, and they were the same to the other girls who were like us. Emily drank it all in, an' tha's why she don't like people, because people weren't nice to 'er mama."

"All the more reason for me to tek 'er out of 'ere, but who is to help us?"

Mary Lucas was not to get her second chance at making a life for herself. An epidemic of typhoid swept through the workhouse, and her name was entered on the Dead List one warm September morning. Her last words had been a prayer:

"Lord Jesus, please please take Emily to the warmth of a family and a home!"

Emily was now alone. She was miserable. She went about doing her little chores daily and learning simple needlework and cleaning. She was in the Girls' Section now and though she kept to herself mostly, she had a few friends, all of them more outgoing than she, who made friends with her rather than she making friends with them.

SCHOOL?

Mr Coates, the new master of Yellowhill Workhouse, soon began to make his views known to the Board. At the meetings, he was cautious enough, showing the Governor and the patrons his account books, and the book of infractions and punishments. There were a great deal of the latter and the Governor questioned why it was necessary to lock up a 70-year old man in the cellar for two days on a diet of bread and water? He defended himself.

"I inherited a very lax establishment, gentlemen," he said. "That pauper you allude to was the ringleader of a group of men who at every opportunity sought to usurp my authority. Since I took that step, Mr Parkes has behaved."

Mr Parkes had behaved because he was laid up in the Infirmary with inflammation of the lungs from a cold caught in the cellar, but there was no need to mention it.

The vicar found out about it later however, when he was asked to visit the old man. He went to the master's office afterwards.

"The cellar in no way caused the lung condition," blustered Mr Coates. "He always had bad lungs, I'm told."

"Then there was all the more reason you should not have punished him thus," Mr Somerset said. "Now I wish to enquire of you, Mr Coates, if there is to be a school for the children."

"Who said anything about the children being schooled?" he asked belligerently of the Vicar. "Is there a law or something?"

"There is, Mr Coates. The Poor Law of 1834," Somerset replied. "I should have thought you would have heard of it, as it has been in effect for many years now. Three hours a day is recommended for boys and girls."

"Pshaw! Stuff and nonsense! Paupers! School indeed! Treated better than the children of hardworking people! It pays to be a pauper nowadays!"

"I venture to say, Mr Coates, that many paupers are very hardworking people, who through some misfortune –"

"Stuff and nonsense!" bawled the Master. "Lazy, the lot of 'em. I won't suffer laziness here in my establishment. Men will break stones and pick oakum and grow food, women will cook and sew and housekeep and pick oakum in their spare time, and the children –" he stopped suddenly, as the vicar's face registered disapproval.

"I daresay there will be a school," he said loftily. There was no sense in making an enemy of the vicar. There would be a school. He would not have it said that there was no school.

As for the troublesome vicar, a word to his cousin *'the member'* about his unsuitability could be conveyed to the Bishop, and Reverend Somerset could be sent off to another parish and out of his way.

Mrs Simpson gleaned the news somehow and the inmates were very sorry about it. Reverend Somerset heard of the matter from them before the Bishop wrote to him, and did not believe it. When the letter came he had no option but to obey, and nobody else cared enough to oppose Mr Coates' plans for the children.

Teachers were engaged, a master for the boys, a mistress for the girls. But their classes were very poorly attended. Mrs Coates arrived to the classrooms every Monday with a list of children who were too sick to attend.

"Pore little things!" she said with as much false feeling as she could muster. "It's so cold today, Miss Bates, I 'adn't the heart to send those six girls over, and what they 'ave is contagious, an' the others would come down with it. They'll be out for the week, they will. They're tucked up in bed and drinking cocoa. Bless their little hearts! It might be two weeks..."

DRUDGERY

The girls missing from the schoolroom were not tucked up in warm beds sipping cocoa. They were on their way to three seedy hotels near the docklands, where an older girl and a younger were to scrub floors and wash linen and do general work in each establishment. Matron – Mrs Coates – had chosen them herself. Emily was one of them, and the eleven-year old girl with her was Jenny. Tractable and frightened, they submitted themselves to the discipline of a Mrs Flint.

Mr Coates owned numerous slum properties by the docklands and rented them to families. He also owned three small hotels or lodging houses for sailors and day labourers and any others who had sixpence for the overnight stay. His interest in becoming Master of the workhouse was mainly for the supply of cheap labour. 'School' had almost thrown a spanner in the works, but he had got around that particular obstacle.

His wife was an unhappy looking woman whose stern ways belied her true feelings. She possessed a heart, but had kept it carefully locked away when forced to deal with the female paupers and children who were her responsibility. She was afraid that if she softened, she would break.

A pauper attendant came for the girls at the end of the long day and they trudged home after her. Too tired to speak, they ate their supper and then, when there was nobody in the dormitory to overhear, they had their say.

"I hated it," Lynn said. "We got only a bowl of gruel for our dinner, and only a small piece of bread."

"The work is very hard," Amy added. "I got some cheese with maggots for dinner and a cup of water."

Emily was silent. She seemed to be faraway, in a state of shock or distress.

"What about you, Em'ly?"

"There were too many people," she burst out. "Horrid smelly men, and Mrs Flint said she'd beat me if I din't work harder. I was workin' as 'ard as ever I could!"

The girls wept until it was lights out. The following day, and every day for several weeks after, they were required to go and work in the seedy lodging houses.

Emily dreaded it more than the others, for she hated to be among people she did not know, and she would never want to know the lodgers, or Mrs Flint with the hairs growing out of her chin like curly wires, or the tradesmen who called at the door demanding to be paid. She detested them all and kept her head averted and spoke to nobody at all except Jenny, who was as taciturn and angry as she was. She missed her mother and cried for her. Mrs Flint gave her thin chicken broth and a piece of bread at dinnertime but she let the cat, her only friend, take a few licks from the bowl. The cat required nothing of her, but after eating had sat by and began to wash its ears and head and stomach. Emily had never been close to a cat before and she found it cheering and calming to watch him. The cat liked her too and came up to her, rubbing itself against her legs. Had it not been for her furry friend, Emily would have been inconsolable and perhaps run off.

At the end of six weeks, the girls were relieved of their duties, and six more girls were 'sick, in bed and drinking cocoa'. The teacher suspected by now that something was up, but declined to do anything for fear of being dismissed. Jobs were difficult to come by. The male teacher had the same situation and they discussed it together in hushed tones.

Six weeks later it was the turn of the first girls again, and they set off with misery. This time Emily did not get the house with the cat and she was very disappointed. She worked hard in the second lodging house, with Mrs Flint splitting her time between the three places to make sure they were working. The girls were unprotected with only each other for company. At least this time she had an older girl companion who was calm and sweet. Maria prayed a lot and helped the younger girl with her difficult chores. When she was with her, Emily felt more at peace. It was a truly dreadful situation, they were as slaves, sent out to work, not free to leave, and unpaid. They did not even have the satisfaction of handing over their wages to a parent to help feed brothers and sisters.

"Why do we 'ave to go out and work like this, Mrs Coates?" Maria asked one day. She was very brave. "There are very odd people in the lodging houses, horrible men some of them – June had to run from one of them, he was trying to do her some 'arm, he was!"

"But you have to earn your keep," Mrs Coates replied, trying not to feel insulted over the kind of clientele her husband's businesses attracted, and also feeling very uneasy. This pauper, Maria, had joined the workhouse only recently, having lost her family to typhus. She seemed possessed of a grace and serenity unusual for her age and situation.

"How much do you think it costs to keep you in food, and uniforms, and boots, and – the roof over your heads? Without us, you'd be on the streets in all weather. You're not half grateful enough, Maria, and I'm ashamed you would ask such a question." But Maria had touched a raw nerve. Doris had married Mr Coates in great hopes of being happy. When she was young she had played fair with people, even the lower orders, and she had been kind. She had got hardened. It made her sad sometimes. But what was to be done? Her husband was her master too.

But Maria's soft face and gentle expression would not leave her alone, and soon she began to require less of the girls. (The boys were her husband's responsibility). She began to give them little rewards and treats and above all, kind words. She strove to get to know them better.

ANGEL MARIA

All the girls aged seven and over were grouped together in the same building. Some of the older girls mothered the younger, and some bullied them. Maria was motherly.

Mrs Coates did not have a high opinion of the girl Emily Lucas. She was silent and sullen. She kept to herself as much as possible, if that were ever possible in an institution packed with children. Emily did not like to be noticed and the other girls did not include her in games.

But Maria approached her one day.

"Hallo, Emily."

"Hallo." Emily did not raise her head from the ground. She had been walking about, thinking.

"Do you like it here?"

Emily looked up.

"Of course I do. I was born here."

"I wasn't born here. Everything is different on the outside."

"I know. I was there once with my mother. I don't like it – out there. It's full of strange people and streets and it would be too easy to lose your way."

Maria continued to talk and Emily began to melt.

"If you like it here, why are you unhappy?" Maria asked.

"I don't like going out and I don't like the horrid hotel and the drunken men frighten me."

"Me too. They are horrid."

They continued to talk. Emily found her easy to talk to.

Mrs Coates saw how Emily was smiling - smiling! – when she was in the company of Maria Peel. In a rush of generous feeling, she thought she would pair them for working.

It was to bear fruit. Maria looked out for the young girl and insisted they have each other in sight when the drunks were about. They provided safety for each other.

"I think of you like my young sister, Katy," Maria sighed. "She was like you. Sort of sad. But she's happy in Heaven now. But you must cheer up, Emily. My granny used to say that God is with us in our troubles. I pray a lot, do you?"

"Only when we have to recite prayers."

"But that won't do at all! You need Jesus by your side all the time. He's not watching you like a judge, but as your Lord and Best Friend. Talk to Him."

Emily was greatly encouraged by everything Maria had to say. For two years, they had a sweet friendship and work did not seem half as bad when Maria was with her. But then Maria had to leave – she had reached the age at which it was time to become apprenticed, and a place was found for her as a domestic servant in a house, and all the girls were sorry to see her go.

There was none sorrier than Mrs Coates. When Maria had been in residence at the workhouse, it was like an angel had walked among them. Now she had left. The girl Emily was inconsolable, but Maria had taught her that she had to make an effort to be friends with the others, it wasn't right for her to be on her own, they'd like her if she made the effort. So for Maria's sake, she tried talking, and listening, and found friendship at last.

EYES OPENED

The house where Emily's mother had worked in Cotham had gone downhill in the last 10 years. Mrs Loft was growing more and more eccentric and a little paranoid about her neighbours, obsessing about them.

"Mrs Hough has put up a new wall, lower than the one she had; now she can see everything that goes on in this house. That was her intention, of course."

"The Wheelers always pause at my gate to look in. It is not to admire the garden. They will come in someday and ask me for a loan. Just because I'm a widow without children everyone thinks I have oodles of money!"

"The dentist charged me far too much to take out a tooth, I could have done it at home, with you helping me, Sarah."

"Oh no Ma'am, that wouldn't do at all. I hate the sight of blood."

"Ah! I caught you out in something at last, Sarah! I thought you were unflappable!"

And so it went on; she found fault with everybody and everything, and it was her against the world. She stayed in bed most of the day, arrayed in satin nightcaps of various dull colours and wraps and shawls to match draped about her shoulders, giving orders for housekeeping while knitting a lengthy piece of brown rectangle in garter stitch, the purpose of which she had not decided yet. She received her few visitors in her bedchamber with the curtains closed, so as not to be properly seen. She resented that when she felt ill, people told her that she looked very well and it felt as if they were accusing her of malingering.

She only got up when Frederick and his wife visited on the first Sunday of the month. They had luncheon together and chatted for a while before they took their departure and she retired back to her chamber.

But one Wednesday Frederick came unexpectedly, on his own. She received him in her chamber and was a little cross about it.

"Is there anything wrong?" she asked. She did not like her nearest relations to think her ill – they would begin to wonder about her last will and testimony.

"I'm afraid so, Aunt. I have a spot of bother with a debt, and I'm very embarrassed to admit it, but I was taken in by another fellow, a man I trusted, named Gilligan –" his tale of woe wore on and the more he said, the less she believed him. He was looking for five hundred pounds. It was a great sum, he was very sorry, but he had been taken in.

"Have you reported it to the police?"

"Oh yes, but there's nothing they can do; Gallagher is well-known to them as a crook."

"Gallagher, is it? I thought you said 'Gilligan'.

"He goes by several names."

"I see." She kept him on tenterhooks while pretending to think.

"Very well," she said at last, but with great reluctance. "You must return here next week, and I will have it for you."

"Next week? Are you sure?" his cheeks were flaming and his hands sweaty as he drew them down his waistcoat.

"Yes, I'm sure."

But the following day his wife Agnes was unexpectedly announced. She swept into the bedchamber and burst into tears.

"Oh, Aunt!" she wept, standing in the middle of the room, unable to go on as she took off her bonnet and flung it on a chair.

"What is the matter? Fred yesterday, and you today – something is very amiss. I demand to know the story, I demand it. Sit by me and tell me."

And so the truth came out.

"He has not been true to me, ever." Agnes said, wringing her handkerchief in her fingers. "He dallies with the maids! Up until now, he has got away with it, and I never knew a thing. But now – a father has come –"

"A *father?*"

"Yes, the father of one of the maids has come and demanded money for his daughter as he claims she is going to have his child."

Mrs Loft's head fell back upon the pillow and she was speechless.

"He wants five hundred pounds for his daughter's care and for the child's keep. Freddie and I had a dreadful row about it all. He admitted to me that he had been untrue almost from the start of our marriage. He also said – that while he was in this house about ten years ago, he almost caused a scandal. There was a child from that connection."

"Oh my – oh my –" Mrs Loft raised her eyes Heavenward. "Oh my Lord! Forgive me! The maid, Mary Lucas, who I treated with such harshness! She told the truth!"

Mrs Loft called for pen and paper, and wrote a brief but scathing note to her nephew, telling him that she would not pay one penny to him, and if he would supply the name of the servant who unhappily was now in a desperate situation because of him, she would see to it herself, directly.

He need not visit her anymore – he was cut out of her will. He was a scoundrel of the lowest order.

As for the maid long ago – where was she now? Where was the child? Something had to be done about them also.

MR AND MRS LUCAS

Mrs Loft got up directly from her bed, called Sarah, and got dressed. She went to her bureau in the parlour and reached into the back for the names of all the servants she had employed since she had moved into the house upon her marriage.

And there it was – a card with the name of Mary Lucas, of Hayward, Devonshire. Her father was a labourer. She would have to go into Devon to find Mary, for that was the only clue she had as to her whereabouts.

"Sarah, we are going to take a trip," she said. "We shall have to go by the post coach, for it's a matter of urgency and I can't afford a private vehicle. The trains do not run to this village."

"Very well, Ma'am!" Sarah was very surprised, for her mistress went nowhere. When she announced her news downstairs, Cook knew what it was about.

"She's going to put right a wrong that was done to that poor maid," she said.

A day later they arrived in the village of Hayward, and enquired at the Inn where Mr Lucas might be found. They were directed to a narrow lane that wended downhill from the respectable main street, with a row of humble cottages, patches of wild grass and weeds here and there, and hens squawking about the doors. Sarah wrinkled her nose.

"You may go back to the Inn," Mrs Loft said. "I will conduct this business myself." Sarah was only too happy to return to the relative comfort of the Inn at the edge of the village and made her escape.

Mrs Loft rapped on the door, and it was opened by a middle-aged woman, who might once have been pretty, but was now faded and pale. Her expression registered puzzlement as she surveyed the older, superior personage on her doorstep.

"I am Mrs Althea Loft, widow of Captain Loft," she said, "I have travelled this day from Bristol. And you are Mrs Lucas, I suppose."

"Well – yes, that's me, Mrs Lucas, wife of Henry." Several children had gathered around Mrs Lucas and stared at the stranger with wide eyes that seemed to fill their none-too-clean faces.

"I am looking for Miss Mary Lucas, who was in service to me at one time," were her next words.

"Go and get your father," Mrs Lucas instructed the oldest child of the gang, who with two more set off, brushing past Mrs Loft as she stood at the doorway, their faces alive with excitement at the unusual visitor with a high hat and a feather in it.

"Won't you come in then?" Mrs Lucas stood aside to allow her guest to pass. It was dark within, the small windows let in only a little light. Mrs Lucas scooped up a red hen that had wandered in and deposited it outside before she shut the door.

"Is your daughter Mary here?" Mrs Loft enquired, her eyes becoming used to the shadows of the dark room. There was a smell of sourish milk in the air and of sticks burning in the fireplace. There was a well-scrubbed table, a few chairs and a flagstone floor. A chipped white dresser held cups and plates.

Mrs Loft was invited to sit in the chair by the fire and the woman of the house threw a stick upon the flames, causing a shower of sparks to explode, one of which landed on Mrs Loft's boot. She hastily drew herself back, frowning.

"Is Mary here?" she repeated crossly.

"No, she isn't here. And she's my step-daughter. Her mother died."

39

The door scraped open and Mr Lucas, a stocky man of middle height, came in. Mrs Loft vaguely remembered him from before when he had escorted Mary to Bristol to take up her situation. He seemed to think she was a brothel-keeper and had wanted to inspect her accommodations, for many young girls were lured to this seaport town with the promise of domestic service but were instead thrown into a world of vice.

"I pray you will be at ease, my good man. She will come to no harm in this house." She remembered herself saying.

"You're looking for our Mary," he said abruptly. There was a smell of tobacco and the farmyard about him.

"Yes, if you would kindly tell me where she can be found, I would like to speak with her."

"We don't know where she is. We 'aven't seen 'er for above ten years, nor 'eard from 'er."

Mrs Lucas spoke. "She came back, but" she raised her voice suddenly "—

go away outside and play, Harry, and take Lucy and Amelia with you!" The children had followed their father inside and were listening intently.

"But she was sent away again," Mrs Lucas finished. "I saw 'er, for I lived up the road then, and saw 'er coming and going."

"She brought disgrace on us. We're good people. She was ruined, in your house. You told me she'd come to no 'arm, and she was ruined there," Mr Lucas said, his voice raised.

"And she returned home and you sent her away. Where did she go?"

"Back to Bristol. She got the early train. I 'aven't heard from 'er since. Her mother died of a broken 'eart, she did."

"So you don't know what happened her, or to the child?"

"She's dead to us," Mr Lucas said brutally. "She disgraced us. Another neighbour saw 'er too, and spread a rumour, and we couldn't hold our heads up here for a year or more. And it was your kin, Mary told us, as promised to marry 'er, and threw 'er over. Your nephew!"

"But how callous of *you* to throw her out! Her own father! Dead to you, you said!"

"We wouldn't 'ave 'ad to throw 'er out if you 'adn't thrown 'er out first," Mr Lucas said. "Your nephew should've stood by 'er. He should've married her! He 'ad his fun and left her desperate."

Mrs Loft rose to go.

She turned around at the door.

"If I find her, do you wish to know?" she asked.

"If she 'as the child with her and she's not married, she can't come back 'ere. Our other children, we 'ave to think of them, and their prospects. There's our 'Arry, the master wants 'im to stay in school and be a teacher."

"Just let us know she's orright," Nellie said. Her eyes were sad.

Mrs Loft swept out. Her thoughts were angry, muddled, and ashamed. It was raining and mud was swirling down the laneway.

She picked her way back to the Inn.

THE SEARCH FOR MARY LUCAS

Mrs Loft hated writing letters, and completely cured now of whatever ailment she had had for years, she trawled Bristol and its environs for her former servant. She visited Maternity Homes, Charity Hospitals, and last of all – the workhouses. She hoped that Mary had not ended up in one of those dreadful places. There was the case only lately in the newspaper about Andover where inmates were fighting over animal bones in order to gnaw any remaining flesh from them, and then Huddersfield was exposed as being overcrowded and full of disease...scandal after scandal emerged from those places, the last resort of the desperate, and many paupers waited until they were in a condition beyond any medical remedy before they succumbed to the humiliation of being admitted there.

But there was no other recourse open to Mrs Loft now, she had exhausted searching the more respectable charities for the poor, and she began her trek to the workhouses.

Her heart leaped with relief when she heard there was a Mary Lucas at the first one, but upon seeing the old, bent woman she shook her head. There was no fruit from three more – how many workhouses were there in the Bristol area? She had come to detest the high walls, the officious porters, the Masters and Matrons who were invariably sent for to investigate what she wanted. Three more Lucas females were found – not the right age, and none of them a Mary.

"We have an Emily Lucas," said one mistress. "She's a poor shy little thing, about twelve years old."

Emily! Frederick's sister's name – was it possible –? A check on her date of birth revealed that the date fit in with Mrs Loft's calculations. And the mother's name had been Mary.

"Where is Mary?"

"She's dead many years."

"The child grew up here?"

"Yes, and likely to stay here for another two years, for she is to be apprenticed as a domestic servant."

"Mrs Coates, I am here to tell you that you need not concern yourself with her welfare from now on. The child is a relative of mine; I will take responsibility for her."

Mrs Coates did not require any confirmation or even evidence that Mrs Loft was a relative. It so happened that Emily was out working, and would Mrs Loft come back on the morrow?

"No, I shall wait here." Mrs Loft planted herself upon a chair.

SUDDEN ALTERATION

Emily was very tired when she returned from the docklands that evening. She was very hungry and wanted to eat supper and looked forward to lying down and closing her eyes in the small, hard bed she shared with another girl.

"Emily Lucas," Mrs Coates was before her the moment she entered the gates. "Come this way. Girls, go on. Emily will not be in for supper."

Emily looked anxiously at the departing backs of her friends as she followed Mrs Coates into the administration building into a room she had not been into before. She looked dumbly at her, lost for words, her eyes requiring explanation.

"You are leaving us," Mrs Coates said, as she summoned an attendant to her side. "Get her some clothes, Bertha."

Emily felt that her stomach turned upside down. She had a dry feeling in her throat. Her head felt light.

"Not now?" she managed to say.

"Yes, now."

"Why?" she stammered. "What have I done? I'm too young for service! Am I not too young?" Possibilities popped into her head – perhaps she was not too young after all and she would be a domestic in a stranger's cold scullery, or perhaps she was bound for a prison cell for some imagined crime, or was it a transfer to another workhouse?

"You're no longer eligible for parish relief," Mrs Coates informed her. "There's a relative here to claim you. Get her ready, Bertha." Mrs Coates left then, and Bertha, with a sigh of impatience, put hands on her and stripped her out of her uniform and pulled and pushed her limbs into street clothes. Emily protested over and over that she did not have any relatives and that there must be some grave mistake.

"Your feet!"

She stuck them out one by one and Bertha dragged her boots off and squeezed her feet into a good-looking, smaller pair. They were too tight.

She then pulled a cloak roughly about her, and a bonnet down upon her head, tying the ribbons tightly under her chin. Emily looked desperately around. She was leaving.

Leaving home forever, for she knew that when the Board of Guardians found a relative to support a pauper, that person had to leave there and then. It had happened to one of her friends.

"Go on then to the porter's office," Bertha was saying. "I 'ave to go now, I'm late for my supper as it is an' I'll only get the dregs an' it's all because of you."

And she was alone. She dragged her feet as she made her way to the porter's office in the archway. Mrs Coates was there with a strange old woman.

"There you are, then. This is Emily Lucas." Mrs Coates told the woman.

"Emily. I am your Great-Aunt Althea. You are coming to live with me."

Emily found no words. Her head spun. Her world had become unreal, as if this was happening to somebody else. In the dining hall her friends were eating supper and talking, then there would be night prayers and then a welcome sleep until morning. Suddenly she wanted to run back in through the archway and to the people she knew.

But she could not. Great-Aunt Althea, a complete stranger to her, was to take her away to a strange place and strange people. Who was this thin old woman, with a high hat with a feather and a black cloak, and with beady eyes boring into her?

"Well come now, Emily." The woman put her arm on her shoulder and steered her toward the door, out to the archway, and onto the street beyond. "The porter has kindly called us a cab already, and it is waiting."

Emily put one foot painfully in front of the other and went to her fate.

IT'S A DREAM, A DREAM.

The motion of the carriage made her feel ill, and it was lucky there was nothing in her stomach to come up. Great-Aunt Althea asked her questions; she managed to mumble answers. Did she remember her mother? Yes. That was good. She died too young, her mother. Did her mother ever speak of her father?

"She said he had gone away," muttered Emily. The carriage sped up and she cried out. "Where are we going?"

Her tone must have sounded desperate, for the woman said:

"There's no need for alarm, Emily. Doubtless everything is strange to you. I am your father's aunt. Yes, he is away, and shall not return to you, but I shall take care of you. You will be happy with me, I hope."

Something in the woman's tone betrayed a little concern, and it did not go unnoticed by the frightened girl. She felt slightly reassured, but only very little. She was too unhappy. At last they reached their destination, a town house on a street with tall buildings. They disembarked, and the front door was opened by a bent old man.

"Michael, this is Miss Lucas. Tell Sarah to air the bed in the blue room and light a fire there, and she is to run a bath."

Miss Lucas? *Who is Miss Lucas?* Was there another Lucas in this house? But it was her they were talking about. *This is Miss Lucas.* Emily came out of her reverie to answer her aunt's question of whether she was hungry.

"I am very hungry, I have worked all the day long."

"Worked all the day long! What doing?"

"Scrubbing and cleaning."

It was suppertime, of course. She sat in a room at a big table adorned with flowers and candles and an array of fine china. But it was not supper. It was a feast like Christmas, consisting of soup (she was served, by the old man) and a roll of white bread on a side plate.

"Are you not going to butter your bread, Emily?" the old woman asked kindly. "There is the butter in front of you. Take your knife – the smallest one – and help yourself to butter."

She had never buttered bread before but did as instructed as the old woman was doing and then she took a bite. The soft white bread and the yellow butter tasted out of this world. What a wonderful meal this was, though the soup tasted different from the soup she was used to, it was thick and creamy!

"Use that spoon for the soup, Emily. Watch me, do as I do."

"Yes, Ma'am."

When her bowl was taken away she thought that the meal was over, and was getting up the courage to ask if she could rest somewhere, but a very large plate was laid in front of her. The old man then placed several slices of hot cooked meat upon it with tongs, then came back with mashed potatoes and peas. Emily was transfixed.

"Well my dear, sit up straight, and eat your roast beef," her great-aunt said. "And call me Aunt Althea. It would please me very much. Copy me, my dear, in the matter of choosing your knife and fork – no not that butter one this time, the other larger, is for this course."

Emily had never tasted food like this meat, ever. She ate everything slowly and wondered if she was going to be sick.

"Did you enjoy it?" Aunt Althea asked, smiling indulgently, waiting for her to finish at last. "Now will you have pudding?"

Emily looked at her in amazement. A plate of creamy white rice pudding was placed in front of her, with a spot of red jam in the middle. She ate it, then felt such a sleepiness come over her that her eyes began to close.

"Of course, you must be very tired – I shall take you to your room, then."

The old man pulled out the chair she was sitting on and Emily got up and followed the woman. She hesitated; there was a roll in the basket on the table. But the old man would see her taking it, so she left the room and followed the old lady up the carpeted stairs. Her hand touched the wallpaper of large green leaves and red flowers. Her aunt was very, very rich. This must be a palace.

Mrs Loft had not envisaged what exactly she would do when she found Mary Lucas, but she thought that she would bring her to her home for a while, and give her money, and set her up in an apartment with her child, if the child was with her. As soon as she found out the way everything lay, it became clear to her that she must take the child to live with her.

"Your bath, Miss Emily." Sarah was standing in front of a great tin bath filled with warm water in front of a fire. Emily was far too afraid to object, though she felt very awkward. Sarah turned her back and Emily quickly undressed and got into the warm, sudsy water. Heavenly! Then there was a clean, warm white towel –

not damp, not grubby, not threadbare – she had never seen a clean towel in her entire life, and this one was as soft as a feather! She was almost afraid to use it, and only that Sarah might turn around at any moment she would have continued to stare at it, so she dried herself as quickly as she could. She was given a long nightgown that felt like silk against her skin, and led to a four poster bed in what to her was a room from a fairy tale castle, though most people would have thought it very old-fashioned and drab.

It's a dream, she thought. A dream. Snuggling under the covers, she fell asleep instantly.

FIRST DAYS IN A NEW LIFE

S he did not know where she was at first when the sunlight streamed in the window and a strange woman was in front of her with a cup and saucer in her hand.

"Tea, Miss Emily, sit up." Sarah put the tea on the night table and plumped the pillows behind her. She then handed her the tea and disappeared. A fire crackled in the grate.

This was true then. While last evening had seemed like a dream, today proved it was real.

A strange world. A world of ease and luxury. But a world where she did not know anybody, and nothing familiar was about her. Today, she was frightened. Her hand shook the cup, spilling the tea into the saucer. She'd never had a saucer under her cup, but she had seen pictures.

Did she not have to go to work today in the docklands, scrubbing floors and peeling vegetables and cleaning out the ashes of the fire? Did she not have to be hungry anymore? Or cold in the dormitory, where there was no fire, not even in winter?

The door opened and Sarah came in again to tell her to get up and to help her to dress, which she was well capable of doing herself, but she did not want to object.

The day passed in a whirl of new, strange things and experiences. Emily felt she ought to be very grateful at the end of it for her full stomach and her visit to the dressmakers and all the new clothes she was to get and grateful too for her aunt's attention, but it was all very overwhelming and her head was full of her aunt's voice who had not stopped talking *all day* telling her things and instructing her, all very kindly, but it was relentless. The voice droned on and on and she could not get rid of it even when she closed her eyes that evening. And her stomach began to feel sick. It took her longer to get to sleep until her aunt's voice faded in her mind.

The following morning, she brought up her breakfast of creamy porridge, poached eggs and toast on the dining-room carpet.

She stood looking at the mess, horrified that she had done such a thing. She would get a beating.

"I'm sorry!" she gasped.

"Oh my goodness!" Aunt was on her feet in an instant. "Why did you not tell me you were feeling sick –?" then her voice softened. "Never mind, dear, too much rich food, I would say, too soon. You have never eaten like this before, have you?"

"No," Emily said miserably, feeling very ungrateful and ashamed, and waiting for someone – the old man maybe – to beat her, or maybe she would be dragged down to the cellar and left there all day in the dark.

"Never mind, dear. It's my fault. I should have known. Sarah will clean it up."

She was astounded. *It's my fault*, her great-aunt said. There was no punishment! It wasn't even her fault!

In the workhouse, whoever was sick had to clean it up themselves. She was sure that Sarah would dislike her, but Sarah was calm and did not show any resentment as she came with a basin and cloths to mop up the sick.

"Now my dear, we will read this morning," Aunt Althea announced a little later. "You shall read to me."

"I can't read well," Emily stammered.

"Oh my dear is that so? We will have to remedy that."

For the rest of the morning Emily had to endure a lesson in reading and writing. "I see I shall have to tutor you, Emily. You are very behind indeed. A girl of your class –

the class you belong to now – has to read well, and sing and play the piano or have some other accomplishment."

"Play the piano? I should be afraid to touch it." Emily paled. There was a piano in the parlour, a great big thing.

"My goodness, you are afraid of every little thing!"

Emily shrank a little at these words. They were true. Being here was becoming an oppression to her. A part of her longed to go back to the workhouse, to everything safe and familiar, though she admitted to herself that she never wanted to be hungry again and never wanted to go to work in the lodging houses by the docks either and the soft bed was very nice.

"I think we will take a walk instead, Emily."

How could she tell her aunt that she simply wished to go to her room and be quiet there for a while? She put her hand to her head.

"Do you have a headache, Emily?"

"Yes, Aunt."

"Well then you must go to bed."

There! It was simply done! Ten minutes later she was alone, with no sound but the ticking of a clock and the rumblings of traffic from outside. She did not have to hear her aunt's voice and strain to remember every word she was told. She slept deeply.

EMILY'S EDUCATION

Downstairs, Mrs Loft pondered this strange new creature who she had plucked from the workhouse. Bringing up her breakfast this morning had shown her how her body was reacting to the big change in her life, and the headache obviously showed her how her mind was trying to cope with this new world, full of things beyond her, and the necessity of learning. It was all too much for the poor child, too soon. She, Althea, had become over-excited with her find, her mission. She was exhausted also, and she rang the bell and informed Sarah that she too was retiring to bed for the day.

As the days wore on all became easier by degrees. For Emily's youth was helpful in her adaptation. Her new clothes were old-fashioned, for her aunt preferred them that way, but Emily did not mind. She did not see anybody her own age. She missed her friends and was afraid to say so in case her aunt thought her ungrateful or worse – sent her back! For she preferred it here, even if she got things wrong sometimes, like hiding food in her room. Aunt Althea had scolded her, but then asked her if she was afraid she would be hungry? Emily had nodded. It was one of those times she'd felt too ashamed and shy to even speak. Aunt Althea had said, in a nicer voice: *"But you will never be hungry here, Emily, I promise you that."*

Emily remembered that moment for the rest of her life, and turned it over in her mind sometimes, wondering why it had been so important for her to have been reassured. She must have been very hungry before.

Mrs Loft found the change more difficult; but she had put her shoulder to the wheel and was not about to send the child away. The child was good, and when told something once, she remembered. She learned willingly.

She engaged a governess for Emily at great expense to herself, for after a few sessions of teaching her she did not feel able to continue teaching Emily herself. She had exhausted herself for weeks now, and took to her bed as before, leaving Emily to the governess, though avidly interested in her education and upbringing. The governess had to report to her of her pupil's progress every week, and she had to hear Emily read to her. She was improving indeed.

Aunt Althea was very particular about her reading material, for Emily liked to lose herself in stories. Not for her the trash her mother used to read! For Mrs Loft had found some books in her attic, and having glanced at them, knew how Mary Lucas had lost her foolish little heart so readily. She was determined that her ward would not be led down the same path. Emily would be led into reading which was good for her.

DANCING LESSONS

"There, you do like piano," Miss Browne was pleased. Her charge's fingers were slender and long and she showed a natural aptitude as she played her first song, a Scottish air. She had a good voice too.

Her days were filled with learning and healthy activities. She and Miss Browne went for walks and nodded to the neighbours. Aunt Althea did not mix with society, and saw no necessity for Emily to do so either. Miss Browne was adequate company, her teacher and her friend. In middle age, she was almost as old-fashioned as Mrs Loft and was rather clueless about modern inventions and new fashions were unknown to her.

Weeks turned into months, months to years, and Aunt Althea's health was failing. There were few if any visitors to the house, and the little family led a secluded life. Emily tended to her great-aunt, pleasing her greatly with her affectionate attentions. They had grown fond of each other.

"You are growing beautiful, my dear." Aunt Althea said to Emily on more than one occasion.

Emily did not believe her. She was sure she wasn't beautiful at all. Not like the other young ladies of Bristol she saw on her walks, who were the height of elegance and fashion. None of them wore spectacles as she was forced to wear, for she was short-sighted. She was taller than most of the other females her age and that made her conscious of herself.

All old people think young people handsome, she thought after receiving another compliment. *Our skin is free from wrinkles, and that makes us prettier than we are in reality. No, I am not beautiful. My mouth is too large; my nose is long. My eyes are nice, but the glasses hide them. And I'm too tall. I'm sure I will never get into the scrape my poor mother did.*

Then Aunt Althea began to ponder what would become of her great-niece after she died, which she felt would be soon. She was in debt, the house and its possessions would be taken by the bank, but she had managed to secure money for her great-niece so she would not be in want.

She will not know how to spend it, she thought. She will be foolish with it and not know what to do. If only I could launch her in society! I have neglected my duty there, but perhaps it is not too late. An idea began to form in her mind and the more she thought of it, the more appealing it became.

Althea had a distant cousin in London. She was a young widow, and very partial to society, moved in high circles, and loved to collect people around her. Young people in particular. Lydia Darcy would be delighted with a lovely young Miss like Emily.

But Emily did not dance! It was highly unlikely that she could recommend herself to any eligible man without that skill. That had to be remedied without delay. And Emily found herself in a public classroom for the first time since she had left the workhouse, but with a difference, they were in a large room without desks or chairs, and a woman played the piano as the master wove himself between the dancing couples in a country dance, calling out the instructions to the group, correcting mistakes, issuing instructions. "Not yet, Mr Rossiter; Miss Young, pay attention."

Her natural aversion to strangers rose as she contemplated the young people there, male and female, being put through their paces.

"I don't like it," she complained to Miss Browne. But the dancing master was coming over to them, all smiles, and bowed. Miss Browne went to sit near the pianist while she was led away to her fate.

She felt awkward and shy as he led her to a young man who was to be her partner for the first practice. He was stony-faced and grumpy and did not appear to be enchanted with his partner and said nothing at all. Her next was a bit better, at least he smiled once, though he can't have been more than fifteen and didn't come up to her chin.

Two of the girls, vivacious and pretty, had swarms of young men around them in the intervals between dances, including her stony-faced partner, who was now clearly enjoying himself. Other girls got into groups – they evidently knew each other well.

I don't attract a swarm, Emily thought good humouredly as she stood awkwardly by the wall. And if I did, I'd probably become anxious and not know what to do. But I would like to speak with somebody instead of standing here looking stupid. She looked about and wondered if she should approach a group of girls chattering nearby, but the task seemed as difficult as breaking into a well-fortified castle.

She went to classes once a week, practicing the steps at home with the assistance of Miss Browne, but she hated the classes themselves. Nobody was interested in talking to her, and she did not put herself forward.

"I dislike company," she complained to her governess when the latter tried to pry her out of her reserve.

"And I'm afraid it shows," Miss Browne sighed. "You wear an expression as if you are in a long queue on the street and it's pouring rain on top of your head. You should smile. People are not ogres, you know. You have to let people know by your demeanour that you are open to being introduced. If you stand by and scowl, nobody will like you."

"I'm not scowling; it's my natural expression when I'm in company."

"But you must alter it then. Think happy thoughts. What do you think about?"

"I think how I don't know anybody and I'm wondering if I look very odd."

Miss Browne was sufficiently concerned to take the matter up with her employer, who listened with a furrowed frown on her brow.

"I should have sent her to school, sent her at fourteen," Mrs Loft lamented. "She's behind others her own age and has not learned the art of conversation. There is little I can do about it at this stage."

GREAT-AUNT'S PLAN

E mily was fully informed of Mrs Loft's plans for
her, and she was appalled. She did not wish to
go to London, a big strange city to live with this
Mrs Darcy, who she had never met in her life, and
imagined to be highly fashionable and very snooty.

Mrs Loft was adamant however. She would go to London.
It was by far the best plan and she was writing a letter to
her cousin.

After she had rescued her great-niece from the
workhouse, she had written to Devonshire to inform the
Lucas' of Mary's death and gave them the news also that
she had their granddaughter living with her in Bristol. She
had never heard a word from them. As Emily had grown,
she had become naturally curious about her relatives.

Mrs Loft had not known what to say at first. She had
invented several stories to herself about an intended

marriage sabotaged, or a marriage that took place, fearing the girl would be horrified at the thought of being illegitimate. But she decided on the truth, and to her surprise Emily did not seem to mind that she had been born out of wedlock to her maidservant and to her own nephew, who was unlikely to ever acknowledge her.

"I knew several children like me," she had reminded her great-aunt, as if it were somewhat normal. Mrs Loft hid her shock. There was a side to life she was utterly ignorant of and her status in life had shielded her from it.

Frederick had sailed to the colonies years before, where he and his wife had intended to make a fresh start, there was no prospect of his returning, nor did she wish him to. As for the Lucas side, Mrs Loft feared that Emily might be tempted to go to them, and any money she gave her would be squandered by them. She had no regard for them.

The best thing for Emily would be to get a husband to love and maintain her, and children to gladden her heart, and the best way for her to achieve that was to go and stay with Mrs Darcy in Cavendish Square, and she took pen to paper.

COUSIN LYDIA DARCY

Mrs Darcy did not care to receive her letters at breakfast, she liked to go onto her Italian-style back patio to read them. On this mild October morning her butler Mr Sallins brought her correspondence on a silver tray with a silver letter opener.

"Thank you, Sallins."

The first two were bills. She frowned at them and set them aside. A third was her bank, gently reminding her of her overdraft. She set that aside too.

The fourth had a childish hand. She opened it without emotion and read the short note.

Dear Mama, I hope this finds you well. I got first in French and Mademoiselle Latour said my accent is very good. You have not come to see me since last May. When will you come to see me?

Please Mama, can I come to you for Christmas? I would rather be with you than go to France with the Alcotts. I am frightened of water.

Your loving daughter, Daphne.

She set that aside and took up the fifth letter. It was postmarked Bristol. It was probably that old cousin she had there. Perhaps she had died and left her money! But the hand was womanly and a trifle spidery, not the careful copperplate hand of an attorney. She opened it, curious.

Dear Cousin, you will be surprised to hear from me, and you must excuse my neglect of you, but since you have not written to me for many years, I suppose we are equally guilty.

To get to the point of my missive, I have a proposition to make you. I have living with me my great-niece for some years now. She is a beautiful girl of seventeen, with gentle manners and possessed of a delicate grace. Due to my age and infirmity I am unfortunately unable to bring her out in society. I therefore request of you to give her a season in Town. I will provide you with a goodly sum of money, if I could trouble you to see to her wardrobe. As I am ill, I cannot see to anything of the sort; in any case I could not guess as to what the fashions are. I will send with her the sum of one thousand pounds. She is to get another sum when she is twenty-five. Should you be in a position to grant my request – and I hope you will answer in the positive - I am so bold as to make another – my manservant is elderly and not up to the task of escorting Emily to Town, so I would be very grateful if you could send a servant for her. I will of course pay all expenses.

Here, Mrs Darcy paused. She had a bronze horse ornament given to her once by a lover, it was supposed to have magical powers, and she took it into her hand and asked it if she should accept.

"But of course," was the answer to her mind. "There are these bills, and the bank notices are getting tiresome, and I can outfit any damsel for a few dinners and balls for only a few hundred pounds, and the rest..."

She returned to the letter.

It is my wish that you will introduce her to some eligible young men of your acquaintance, of good character, and that if an attachment develops on her side that you will do all you can to further it.

Why does Cousin Loft think I know young men? She was annoyed but then laughed.

The butler had entered the patio again and was before her.

"Mr Anthony Jennings is on the doorstep, Madam. Are you at home?"

"No, I am decidedly *not* at home. Tell him I have not risen yet and cannot see anybody."

"Yes, Madam."

The butler returned a few minutes later with a bunch of red roses.

"Just do the usual with them, Sallins."

"Yes, Madam." The usual thing was to give the flowers from yesterday's lover to Mrs Sallins, his wife who was housekeeper, for their own apartment.

"Poor Mr Jennings is besotted," Sallins said as he handed them over to his wife who was in the still room. She threw her eyes upwards.

"Another one. What age is he, do you think?"

"Not more than twenty-three, I would say."

"She tired of him very quickly. She really ought to find a man who is her own age, or older."

"But that could give away her true age!"

The bell rang in the patio and Coffey the footman went to answer it.

"She wishes to see you, Mr Sallins," he said when he returned.

Sallins went again to the leafy, fragrant area adorned with Milanese tables and chairs. A bird sang somewhere. His mistress looked up from her correspondence.

"Sallins, I have been meaning to speak with you about that footman. Coffey."

"What of him, Madam?"

"He is nowhere about, is he?"

"No, Madam. I set him to a task in the pantry."

"It is this – I do not think he belongs in this establishment."

"Why not, Madam? His work is very satisfactory."

"Perhaps so, Sallins – but he does not fit in. His mien, his swarthy complexion – his disfigured face –"

"He had smallpox, Madam."

"Yes, well, I'm glad he lived. But I can't stand the sight of anybody in this establishment who does not present a good appearance before me and my guests. The footman serves drinks and aperitifs, and serves at table also. His probationary period is up very shortly, I understand?"

"Yes, Madam. In three weeks."

"Sallins - I want you to send him away with a glowing character. Perhaps an older person with her sight fading may welcome such a face, but not me." She laughed at her own joke. "A footman has to have a good appearance, Sallins." There was a reproach there, but Madam did not know that the footman was a relative of his wife's.

"As you wish, Madam." Sallins kept his voice neutral. "Will that be all, Madam?"

"No, there is something else. A far-out relation is about to spend the autumn and winter here. She is Miss Lucas from Bristol. I shall be giving dinner parties and perhaps even a Ball to honour this young lady. And I shall send you to fetch her, as there is apparently nobody to take the charge in Bristol, except the antiquarian male servant my cousin keeps who has probably never travelled by train."

"I shall be happy to take the charge, Madam."

His wife knew something was amiss when he returned. He drew her aside to tell her about the footman who did not please Mrs Darcy.

"What shall I tell his mother? I hope you and I pass muster, Mr Sallins," was her next anxiety. She swung about to look in a small mirror on the wall and frowned.

"Be at ease, Mrs Sallins. We have been called uncommonly handsome, both of us," he said, peering at the reflection of himself.

"So you will have to get another footman. A handsome one."

"It seems so. I have the unpleasant duty of telling poor Coffey he is dismissed. What shall I tell him?"

"Tell him that Madam has to turn off some servants due to financial retrenching."

"That will have to do. He was last in, so first out. Thankfully the maids have clear complexions and pretty figures and features, and not likely to offend her very particular sensibilities."

"Oh so you have noticed, Mr Sallins, have you?" she bantered.

"My dear, you are superior to all of them," he reassured her. "Oh! I nearly forgot! Madam has news that will interest you." He related the interesting intelligence.

"What if this newcomer puts her eye on one of Madam's bachelor paramours?"

"Or if the paramours prefer the younger lady!"

"We shall be vastly entertained, Mr Sallins!"

"This is a jolly house," said the butler. They had only joined the family six months before. "I am to go to Bristol to fetch Miss Lucas. She had better be handsome or Mrs Darcy will try to be rid of her."

TROY'S STORY

"**T**roy!"

'There he goes again,' the young footman thought.

"Yes, Mr Jameson?"

"You are not to be trusted with the keys to the cellar, Troy."

"I beg your pardon, Mr Jameson?"

"There are two bottles of wine missing."

"I didn't take them, Mr Jameson."

"If you didn't, who did?"

Troy was quiet for a moment, preferring the butler to come to this conclusion all by himself, but the older man kept looking at him, a frown upon his brow. Troy sighed to himself.

"Probably somebody else with access to the cellar, sir!"

The truth dawned upon Jameson and he told the young footman he might go.

Troy was indignant. The young sons were always getting him into trouble, for the butler thought the young men of the house were model gentlemen. Master Cullen had had the key of the cellar copied, he was sure, and used it at will to pinch wine for himself and his friends. Last month the back door had been left open; the butler blamed Troy for opening it after he had locked it for the night, but that was young Master John, who had sneaked out. He was not even safe from the girls. Miss Cullen had called him to the parlour on a silly pretext to show him off to her visiting school friends like a prize pug. Her friend was at the piano and as soon as he had appeared the friend had launched into a lively Viennnese waltz. Miss Cullen had come right up to him, placed her hand on his shoulder and said: "Shall we dance, then?" expecting him to place his hand around her waist to lead her in a waltz. Troy had blushed furiously, excused himself and left the room, and later received a reprimand from her mother saying that he might have obliged her daughter, who was embarrassed and could not understand his odd behaviour, for the girls simply needed to practice the waltz, and he had read too much into it, etc, etc.

Why din't I just say I din't know how to waltz, Troy said grimly to himself. *I never think of these things until afterwards!*

Even the youngest Cullen was a source of trouble. Yesterday, little Miss Gail lost her ball and her governess told him to search the hedge at the back, and he didn't hear the front door knocker and found himself in trouble once again.

I'm gettin' the blame for everythin' around 'ere, he muttered to himself. *Blimey! Someday there'll be a burglary and I wouldn't be surprised if Johnson had me arrested for it!*

He was polishing the railings outside when the young master swaggered by.

"Morning, Troy!"

He did not reply.

"Oh, we're uppity, are we?"

"Your escapades are getting me into trouble with the butler, sir."

"Oh dear! Escapades!" He mocked and took the steps in one bound up to the front door.

That did it. He would wait no longer. Later that day he took a discarded newspaper and looked in the 'Help Wanted' section, scanning it for situations suitable for himself.

FIRST FOOTMAN WANTED; OF GOOD APPEARANCE AND CHARACTER, TO WORK IN GOOD HOUSE, LIVERY AND BEER, MUST HAVE EXPERIENCE.

There were others he applied for with similar requirements.

He handed in his notice and asked for a character, which he got and it was more satisfactory than he expected.

He had his interview with the butler of his preferred situation in a respectable public house where they sat at a table and had a beer. His name was Mr Sallins. There was only one family member to be pleased in this house, a widow of means in Cavendish Square. An old widow, he thought, assuming like most people that being widowed implied advanced age. *Nobody likely to get me into trouble then.*

"She likes to entertain," said Mr Sallins.

"Suits me, sir."

"You present a good appearance, certainly. What height are you, Troy?"

"I don't rightly know that, but I could be called tall I suppose."

"And you are from London?"

"Whitechapel, sir. My parents live there. They were in service, both. That's where they met."

"Sixteen pounds a year with food and board?"

"That's more than I thought would be offered, sir."

"My mistress is very generous, Troy. I have said that there is only one in the family, but there is another to join her, a young cousin who will come for the Season, I understand. I'm to go and fetch the young lady from Bristol soon and if you could be engaged by then it would be convenient."

A young lady. Hopefully she would be nothing like the flighty Miss Cullen or any of her friends.

CHANGE IS DIFFICULT

When Mrs Loft beheld the girl she called her ward, she saw large limpid eyes and a striking resemblance to the girl she was called after, Frederick's sister Emily.

Emily Lucas at seventeen presented a rakish appearance, but the other Emily had grown out of that as she had approached twenty, developing a more mature figure. She hoped that this Emily would follow suit. She had angular features and a brownish complexion from the sun. She was not an English Rose, and she habitually forgot her sunhat when she went into the garden during the summer, and a few freckles had settled on her nose and cheeks. She was not in the least vain.

"Aunt won't you change your mind about sending me to London?" she begged. "Who is to see to you here?"

"Sarah is perfectly capable of attending to me, and I shall engage a parlourmaid to take her place. So you see, you are helping Sarah up in the world, for after I die she can call herself a nurse."

"Die! Do not mention the word!" Emily shuddered.

Her aunt was sad but gratified.

"You will soon forget me, and be the talk of London," she said, pleased. "You are the dearest creature in the world and I dread to think how lonely and bitter I would have been had you not come to me."

"You took me from the workhouse, remember, Aunt."

"Yes and a very frightened little creature you were too!"

"I am frightened again now, for I don't like alteration."

"Then it is well past time you left me. You have to have some society. I should perhaps have sent you to school, but I was selfish and got used to having you here, you gladdened my heart. Now, I must get up and make a final trip to the bank, for the money is ready, and you are to take it with you to give to Cousin Lydia for your dress and other expenses involved in launching you upon the world."

This prospect made Emily's heart tremble – she was not at all sure she liked 'the world' and the thought of having to be brought into society, go to dances, balls and dinner parties and to have to say and do everything right was intimidating indeed. Afraid of judgement and social condemnation for her awkwardness, she would have preferred to avoid it altogether. But she said no more.

Together they went to the bank and returned with one thousand pounds in twenty fifty pound bills. The bank had placed it in a sturdy envelope. At home again, Mrs Loft wrote 'To Cousin Lydia, for Emily's Expenses' on the front and enclosed a letter of thanks and some suggestions on how it should be managed and spent. She sealed it. She placed it into a bigger, brown envelope and set it on her dressing table until it was time for the departure.

GOODBYE TO BRISTOL

The dreaded day came, Mrs Loft got up and saw to the packing, advising her great niece about the best way to fold her gowns, and how to protect her clothes from the soles of boots and shoes.

"In truth you do not have very much, and that is my fault – but never mind –

Cousin Lydia will see to you. Now I have that package of bills for you, and you are to carry it with you at all times. Hark! I heard a coach – is that the man Sallins, come to take you? He will have something to eat and drink, and away with you both to the train station. Oh dear, I see that alarmed look in your eye again!"

A knock came to the door, and the butler from Cavendish Square was admitted. Aunt Althea received him alone in the drawing room before she called for her niece.

"Emily, this is Mr Sallins who will convey you to London."

Mr Sallins bowed. His expression was impassive, but he knew, the moment he saw her, that his mistress would not like her. Most of the human race were not either very beautiful nor very ugly, but fell in between in varying degrees. This Miss was a degree too much on the wrong side. Tall, thin, angular-featured and spectacles! She would not do! The next weeks promised diversion for him and Mrs Sallins and the servants.

While Mick took her bags downstairs, Emily took one last look around at her little room. The deep blue rug and curtains, the little table and chair and wardrobe – the floral washbowl and jug, even the paintings on the walls – all seemed to beseech her to stay, taunting her that only new, strange and unfriendly places awaited her. She dropped to her knees and laid her head upon the bed.

"Lord Jesus, if it is Your will, I accept it. But I am very frightened, as if this is going to be a nightmare. Hold my hand, Lord! Why do I dislike the unknown?"

She remembered how she had felt leaving the workhouse. The workhouse! How could she have been sad and afraid leaving such a place? Was it because she had not known, that much better awaited her? But she had been a child then. She was grown up now, and fear was unseemly – she had to conquer it.

She forced a smile and made her goodbyes to Aunt Althea in her room. She kissed her forehead and saw tears gather in the old eyes.

"I can stay, Aunt. Send him back without me."

"No, no. You have no future here. Go now, and be a good girl, and try your best to be friendly with people, and write to me. Remember do not let the envelope out of your sight and carry it close to you. I gave you some sovereigns and coins for your purse, do you have them?"

"Yes, Aunt."

"Go then, there is no sense in prolonging this."

Mrs Anderson, Sarah and Mick were in the hall to wish her well. She embraced all of them, surprising even herself at her own deep feeling.

She gave one look around before she stepped into the cab where Sallins waited. The street had never looked so beloved! She knew every window, every shop front, and even bald Mr Henry, who was in his apron and sweeping his part of the pavement, looked suddenly dear, whereas she had never marked him before. She waved impulsively to him, and he, surprised, waved back and stared.

When the door shut, she burst into tears.

'Well you might cry, young woman, for I doubt you will be happy where you are going', Mr Sallins said to himself, 'in spite of all the money you're carrying close to your chest'. As he

settled her on the train her misery made her look even less appealing, and he escaped to second-class leaving her to her companions in her coach in First.

The farther the train took her from Bristol, the more miserable she felt.

CAVENDISH SQUARE

Lydia Darcy had worked herself into a state of pleasant expectation while awaiting her special guest. She sat in her upstairs dressing room and posted her maid, Mademoiselle Chalamet, at the window.

"Zere is a station cab stopping outside, Madam! And Monsieur Sallins, he gets out! And hands out – a woman, not Miss Lucas, I think, but her maid – ooh a lazy maid, Madam, because she carries no hatbox or anything but her own little reticule, and stands about as if she has nothing to do with the luggage. So tall and thin, like a rake!"

Lydia rushed to the window in time to see the carriage door shut and the cab driver paid.

"She has not come, but sent her maid? Oh! No doubt she is in a carriage behind, with Cousin Althea's own manservant after all, and if I had known I could have been spared the trouble of sending my own butler all the way to Bristol for her, for he was needed here – but never mind."

Downstairs in the cold hall, Emily looked about her at the purple and grey walls and modern furniture with an uncertain look upon her face. Mr Sallins took her bonnet and cloak, and conducted her to the drawing room to await his mistress. A footman appeared, listened to his orders from Sallins, and took her bags upstairs.

Chalamet retired to the dressing room to put away her mending, and Lydia decided to go downstairs to see what was afoot.

Sallins was just on his way up.

"Your charge has arrived, Madam."

"Oh! I did not see her arrive – I saw the maid – well never mind, I shall be down directly."

Sallins smirked to himself, but his face was impassive as always. She must have seen the woman with him, and assumed she was Miss Lucas' maid. What a story for Mrs Sallins!

"She is in the first drawing room, Madam."

"Thank you. We shall eat at eight, Sallins."

A few minutes later Emily startled when the drawing room door opened and a woman swept in, of middle height, dressed in a crinoline gown of coral and white with a very fancy bodice, sleeves and decorations. She had impossibly golden hair under an elaborate lace cap and wore long earrings and a great deal of jewellery besides. She was decidedly a woman of confidence and fashion.

"Oh," she said when she saw the young woman before her, as if taken aback. "You are the maid. Where is Miss Lucas? There is no calamity I hope? She is not ill and gone to her room already?"

"I am Miss Lucas, and I am well, thank you." Emily replied shyly.

"You are Miss Lucas?" It was said somewhat disbelievingly.

"Yes, I am."

"You are not her maid, then?"

"No."

"I saw you arrive out the window and I thought you were Miss Lucas' maid. Do you have a maid?"

"No."

There was a very awkward silence as each took the other in.

'Awkwardly-built, tall girl with nothing to recommend her in her figure. Her mouth's too big for her face. Her nose is too long. Spectacles! She is not what I expected at all. I cannot make a beauty out of that. She has the look of a donkey.'

'So rich and elegant in her dress, but she has a look in her eyes I do not like. A hard look, disapproving of me. I know it. She thought I was a maid! Am I so drab? She does not welcome me. Why did I come here? It's all going to be so horrid. I hate it already.'

"Very well then. I am glad you are in good health. We will eat soon." She pulled the bell and the footman arrived. He was tall, had light brown hair, a rather serious expression and well-proportioned features. He was handsome.

"Troy, be so kind as to conduct Miss Lucas to her room and inform my maid Chalamet to attend her there."

Emily noticed that when he came into the room, Mrs Darcy had relaxed and smiled, the hard look in her eyes melting.

"Are you settling in, Troy?" Mrs Darcy asked the footman.

"Yes, Madam. Thank you." He said no more and turned to leave the room, and Mrs Darcy, the hard look back in her eyes, motioned to Emily to follow him.

She followed him up the stairs, onto a landing and down a passage where he stopped and opened a door.

"Will there be anything, Miss? Besides the maid, I mean – I will inform her now."

"No, nothing at all." Emily froze suddenly, was she supposed to give him a tip? She dug her hand into her reticule and brought out sixpence.

"Oh no, Miss." He drew away, a hint of a smile doing away with the serious look upon his face. "I can't take that for doing my duty. I hope you will be happy here, Miss." He disappeared and she closed the door. She went to the window and looked out on the neat back garden. It was long and pretty, with a lawn, a path, a few fruit trees, rows of neat shrubbery and a carriage house by the back gate. A gardener was working in the shrubs and a little white dog pranced about on business of his own.

A rap at the door followed, and a maid entered, her snowy cap very elaborately arranged upon her head, her chin in the air, her mouth in a thin, hard line.

"I am here to assist your mistress, though since she has you, I do not know why I am required. Where is she, and why are you standing about? Unpack! The drawers are over there!"

"I'm sorry for the misunderstanding – I am Miss Lucas, and I do not have a maid."

"Oh, you are Miss Lucas?" Chalamet looked her up and down and Emily watched as the lady's maid threw open her bags, which she clearly thought inferior, and placed her items in drawers and the wardrobe with some hurry and she thought, resentment.

"Which gown shall you wear for dinner, Ma'am?"

"Oh, I don't know – I suppose the plaid. Yes, the plaid, Charlotte."

"It is not Charlotte. It is Chalamet. That is my surname. You do not call me by my Christian name; that is for lower servants. Now, the plaid." Her tone was condescending.

The maid quickly helped her into the plaid gown and then bade her sit down at the dressing table and none-too-gently took her hair out of their pins and brushed it after a contemptuous look at her hairbrush. She said nothing, except to ask what she wanted done with it, and when Emily replied 'just a simple style – whatever may be easiest" she sighed and gathered her tresses in a simple bun at the back of her neck. The hairpin jabbed her head. She was gone then. Because Troy had refused a tip, Emily did not dare offer it to the maid.

THE POOR RELATION

What to do now, go downstairs again? She took up the very important envelope she was meant to hand to her hostess. She made her way downstairs. Troy was in the hallway. She nodded to him.

"Where is dinner served?"

"In the dining room, Miss."

Of course, that was a stupid question, she thought. He must think I'm a fool.

"And that is –?"

"It is there, Miss, but as she went in the direction of the dining room, he interrupted her.

"Miss," he said in a low, polite tone, "Before dinner, you must go to the drawing room." He strode to a door and opened it for her. She nodded her thanks.

The footman had a friendly, open face. She noticed, in a sort of idle way, that his eyes and hair were almost the same colour, rich light brown. His hair seemed to shine with dashes of gold, or perhaps it was the light flickering in the wall sconces that made it look like that. His livery for evenings was royal blue with red braid on the collar and cuffs.

Her cousin awaited her in the drawing room. Emily entered with a little uncertainty as to where she ought to sit and seeing this, she saw her cousin sneer a little, so she sat in the chair nearest to the door. There was silence. Then Sallins entered to announce that dinner was served, and as they both rose there was a little misunderstanding. Of course Emily would have stood back to allow her to go first, but just in case she did not, Cousin Lydia barked: "I go before you, you know," and swished past her. Emily felt humiliated.

Dinner was formal and elaborate compared to her great-aunts. Mrs Darcy spoke little. If Emily had guessed her thoughts, she would have been very happy indeed, for she was thinking of sending her back to Bristol on the morrow. But Mrs Darcy thought better of that.

"Is that envelope you have been carrying intended for me by any chance?" she asked with some cordiality.

"Yes." Emily felt foolish and handed over the envelope. She had not wished to give it to her with the footman in attendance, feeling it to be a private matter. Her hostess tore open the wax seal and looked at the contents carefully.

She could not send her back – here was a fortune. She needed the money. She re-closed the envelope and set it by her plate

"I am giving a dinner for you tomorrow evening," she said. "You must show me your best gown after dinner. It will have to do for the occasion; of course you will need an entire new wardrobe."

"You've already seen my best gown," Emily said shyly. "I travelled in it."

"That, that maroon? No, that will not do at all."

Emily squirmed.

"This one then?"

"Oh dear no, not plaid! Plaid is for mornings! It is too late to cancel the invitations, so we will have to think of something."

"How many are coming?" Emily felt a sense of dread rising in her breast at the thought of meeting new people.

"Only about thirty, a small group. Did Mrs Loft give many parties or at-homes?"

"None at all."

"You have never entertained, then? But you have gone to parties and dances and teas of course."

"Not many," Emily said, now distressed.

Troy served them and heard all. His sympathies were with the poor young woman who was so oddly out of place in this house. A poor relation, he supposed. She had a quiet, graceful air he admired but behind her spectacles her eyes were sad. She projected a lost look.

TEARS AND TROUBLE

There was merriment in the servant's hall. They had just eaten their pudding, and Chalamet had done a great mimicry of the new young Miss, and everybody was laughing, all but Troy, who thought it was rotten of her to make fun of a shy, timid person.

"I asked what gown she wanted to wear for dinner, and she said:

' "Oh the plaid, it's the only one I have besides this one I travelled in, this maroon thing! Will I get a rich husband in my plaid gown, Miss Chalamet?" '

She did not say that, Troy thought.

"And then – her jewellery – nothing but a few cheap necklaces and bracelets, nothing to admire at all. She has no evening gown, no hat good enough to be out in, nothing fine, and – she – there is nothing light and silky, if you know what I mean –" This was greeted with raucous, shocked laughter.

Disgusting, Troy thought. He got up from the table and went up the stairs, intending to spend a little time there on his own. His first days in service in this house were not promising. The butler and housekeeper did not keep any order among the servants, and allowed them to talk as they wished about anybody. They seemed to find the kind of conversation that had just taken place amusing. There was a shallowness about them.

The raucous laughter continued, and he mounted the back stairs to get away from it. Then he became aware of someone weeping. The sound was coming from above him. He proceeded cautiously toward it, and saw a female figure crouched on a step beside the green baize door, her head in her hands, weeping bitterly. She looked up in alarm when she heard him approach.

"Oh, I'm sorry – I thought you were all at your dinner," she said, flustered and embarrassed. It was the newcomer. She had taken off her spectacles.

"Are you all right, Miss Lucas? Is there anything I can do? Would you like some water perhaps?"

She shook her head and burst into tears again. He considered for a moment, then sat down on the step below hers.

"If there's anything I can do to help you, please tell me," he said.

"There's nothing you or anybody can do. I was sent here, and I do not belong here. I'm going to be desperately unhappy, I am already."

"Come, come, it will get better, Miss Lucas."

"No, it won't. I don't want to go to dinners and parties and balls, the thought fills me with fright! There, I've said it, I'm a failure before I even begin!"

"Miss Lucas, it's just because you're new here. I'm new too. I too wish I had not come here, but gone to another place."

Another burst of laughter reached them from below. Thank God, Troy thought, that Miss Lucas could not hear the conversation from here!

"She expected somebody completely different than me. And if she knew where I spent my childhood, she would send me downstairs as the scullery maid."

"We could talk easier then," Troy said without thinking. Miss Lucas had no airs, and did not mind him speaking to her as an equal. Who was this poor girl? She was out of place here in this fancy house in Cavendish Square! There was an American heiress living not three doors away, and an elderly Countess, and an eccentric Earl.

"You see, my great-aunt probably gave her a wrong impression, and told I was this or that, and I'm not. Miss

Chalamet sneered at everything I had. Oh! You will tell her." She looked at him with wide eyes. It was not quite dark and he noticed that they were lovely eyes; tilted a little upwards at the outer corners and long-lashed, and her eyebrows were swept up at just the same angle. Her cheekbones were high, her lips full.

"I won't tell 'er. I'm just a footman, Miss Lucas." He said gently. "She's a lady's maid and much 'igher than me. And she knows it. Take no notice of her. And just call her Chalamet, not Miss Chalamet."

"You are very kind, Troy. Can – can we be friends?"

He hesitated. How to put this kindly?

"It's not usual, Miss Lucas, for a servant and a lady of the house to be friends."

"But I do so need someone to talk to! And you can advise me on how things are done, and tell me if I'm doing anything wrong, like when I was about to enter the dining room tonight instead of the drawing room. Please, Troy."

She isn't shy with me, Troy thought.

"Just keep an eye out for me, please," she went on. "I would hate to embarrass Mrs Darcy in company. I shan't mind if you give me hints and correct me. You're in service; you know their ways."

"I'll try, Miss."

"My name is Emily!"

"I can't call you that."

"Troy! Where are you?" they were afoot now downstairs, the comedy show was over and they had to go upstairs and clear the dining room.

"You won't say it back to the mistress or to the butler that I wish I had taken another place?" He asked her.

She shook her head. "You keep my secret, and I will keep yours."

He smiled, got to his feet and held out his hand. She took it and he lifted her to her feet. She smiled suddenly; just a simple act of kindness and courtesy had made her smile. She had a lovely mouth and he had a sudden wish to kiss her.

Stop, Troy! This is all wrong! He told himself not to be foolish. But he could not get Miss Lucas – Emily – out of his head for the entire evening.

SECRET FRIEND

"We are in urgent need for a gown for tonight," Mrs Darcy had brought Emily in tow to her mantua-maker. "I'm willing to pay what you ask. What of this one?" She put her eye on an ivory organdie that one of the seamstresses was busy with, sewing roses of purple silk onto the neckline. "It looks nearly finished."

"I'm sorry Madam. I cannot sell you that one. But I have one which is not required anymore – a woman was to call for it six weeks ago, and she never did, and now it is mine to do as I wish with – I am sure that with a little alteration, it will fit the young lady." She brought out a buttercup yellow creation and nodded to Emily.

"It is not a good colour for her sallowness," Mrs Darcy frowned. "But beggars can't be choosers, I suppose."

Emily did not like it. But it was the only one that could be made ready for the evening party, so she endured the dressmaker getting her into it. She could tell that Mrs Darcy was embarrassed at her frayed stays and faded chemise. The neck of the new gown was low, the shoulders exposed. The atmosphere was awkward, she should have been enthusiastic and grateful and she was not.

Troy was waiting outside with the coachman, and he was summoned to carry the package, and they proceeded to a posh shop on Bond St, where fans and hair ornaments and other items were purchased. Troy carried the purchases to the carriage. Not a look or a word passed between him and Emily, though they were conscious of one another. Mrs Darcy bestowed smiles upon him and whenever he was present, she adopted a cheerful and sweet temperament. Emily was serene and calm. The presence of Troy made both women glad, the older one because she wished to appear to advantage; the other reassured at the presence of a friend, a secret friend.

"We must hasten; there is not much time – your hair will have to be simply done. We must see about getting you a maid, or perhaps the parlourmaid can do for you. She has good taste; yes, we will get Stella." There was no requirement to waste money on a lady's maid for Miss Lucas.

Emily was relieved not to have the snooty Chalamet anymore, but Stella proved too curious for her liking.

Where had she come from? Had she a mother and father? Had she a sweet'eart? Emily was evasive with her answers. She rightly guessed that it would be discussed downstairs.

LOATHSOME TRICK

I t was time. Her hair was curled into ringlets – Stella had done her best. She had a head band of white lace and carried a white fan. It was time to go down and face the music. She took a deep breath. She did not feel so nervous – Troy would be there, in and out serving drinks and later serving at table. She was to go now to Mrs Darcy's boudoir and go down with her.

"Remember you are a hostess," Mrs Darcy instructed her. "Remember everybody's name."

That was going to be difficult. She had left off her spectacles and could hardly see beyond her nose.

She curtsied awkwardly to everybody she was introduced to, and tried to remember names. They were a remarkably good-looking set of people, all on the young side; handsome men, elegant women, and they passed into the drawing room and chatted there.

The women were seated, and Emily was one of three ladies upon a sofa, she at one end. She felt strangely mute and shy. The other young ladies appeared to know each other very well and whispered and giggled behind their fans.

There were two young men standing near her, and she could hear their conversation.

"Jennings, out of favour already, are you?"

"What do you mean, Venables?"

"She got rid of you quickly enough tonight, and passed you on to me; how boring for you, when you'd far rather be in her sweet company."

"Shut up, my good fellow. The world will hear you."

"Do you want to know who your successor in favour is?"

"She does not favour anybody now, if it's not me. It's not you, is it? I daresay she has no taste."

"Not me, sir. No, but I shall tell you – we will all be excessively diverted –

it's her new footman!"

Emily pricked up her ears.

"It's not a very good joke."

"I am serious. She told Mrs Brooke that if he were a gentleman, she would be as infatuated as Lady Caroline

Lamb was about Lord Byron. Mrs Brooke was highly diverted and told her husband, who told me. Look, look, the devil himself, here he comes in his best livery with his tray of sherry. Handsome fellow, isn't he? A Greek god. I shall teach him a lesson for you, shall I? How would you like to see him sprawled upon the carpet with his tray of drinks overturned? I shall go near that curtain there, which will hide me, and come out suddenly, and be all apologies."

Jennings began to laugh quietly; Venables moved swiftly away in the direction of the curtain.

Without giving a thought to what she was doing, Emily sprang up and followed Venables.

"Mr Venables," she cried to his back. "I have need of you this moment, do not proceed further, I pray."

There was a lull in the conversation, for she had spoken loudly. Many heads turned in her direction. Venables turned about.

Emily did not know what to do next. Venables was looking at her curiously. Her heart was hammering, but with fury, not fear.

"I am at your service, Miss Lucas." Venables said, inclining his head.

"I wonder if you could – could explain that painting," she said, waving her gloved hand toward a large portrait. Troy passed them by with his tray full of filled glasses, saved from sabotage.

"Er – what do you wish to know, Miss Lucas?"

"Whose portrait is it?"

"It is the Duke of Wellington, of course." He looked a little curiously at her.

"Thank you," she said, blushing, and withdrew. She knew it was the Duke of Wellington, everybody knew the man who had saved England from the mad Napoleon at Waterloo, and she felt silly for asking, but then remembered the reason she had to distract him, and that was the first thing that had popped into her mind.

Troy was in attendance the whole evening, and nothing was done to embarrass him, so Emily concluded that once the opportunity had passed, that Venables had lost interest.

When the guests had left and the servants had taken the tea tray away, Mrs Darcy launched into a diatribe of how awful – *simply awful* – she had been. She had looked so awkward leaving the drawing room on the arm of Mr Venables who took her into dinner, and why did she not talk to him? It was atrocious manners, and they must have felt slighted. She was disgraced. She had hardly spoken a word, except for that odd outburst in the drawing room.

"That was the clumsiest, most awkward attempt at flirtation that I have ever seen. Calling out to him like that! It was the height of vulgarity. You sounded like you were selling apples. You have no idea. Ashton Venables is not available to you, by the way. He is not for you. You embarrassed me!"

"I am sorry!" tears rolled down Emily's cheeks.

"You have so much to learn, and I do not know if I can get a husband for you if you do not have the basic skill of flirting, and as you have no fortune, it will all depend upon your – charms, which I am sorry to say, are in short supply. You forgot names. And you squinted at people."

"Get a husband for me?"

"Yes, that is why you're here! Did your aunt not tell you? She wants you married before the season is out. Perhaps I can find somebody for you who is not too particular. Yes, I'm sure such a man exists, though where to find him, is another matter."

A BALL IS ANNOUNCED

Miss Lucas' social awkwardness continued to provide mirth for the servants' hall. The butler and housekeeper were as amused as anybody. Troy usually left the table when this began. Then they began to talk about him, because he was not there.

"We know where his interests lie, don't we?" Stella said. "He goes upstairs to talk with the mistress in the evenings, for Miss Lucas doesn't sit around and talk. She can't wait to get away from the mistress and she goes up to 'er room. I bet 'e sits in the chair on the other side of the fire, where Mr Darcy used to sit, getting used to it under 'im. What do you know, Chalamet?"

"I am not in the habit of bringing my mistress' business to the servants' hall," the maid replied. "But she has mentioned that her guests, particularly the ladies –

have admired him and congratulate her on her taste. She is afraid that Lady Ferrars, in particular, will try to steal him."

This brought laughter, for Lady Ferrars had stolen several servants from her already.

"'E thinks he's too good for us, anyroad," remarked the parlourmaid Delia from Durham in the north of England. "Gettin' up and goin' away like that whenever anybody says somethin' interestin'! 'E's a snob, 'e is, of the 'ighest order."

Delia had her eye on the new footman. She had come to London two years before and joined the House six months ago. She liked it better than her other places. It was not a stuffy house. The butler and housekeeper loved a good gossip as much as the maids did. She had so much to write home about she filled three pages. It irked her though that Troy did not pay her any attention, for at home she was reckoned to be good-looking.

"There was an invitation to a Ball today," Sallins remarked, looking about him with interest.

"Ooh I wonder what she will wear to that!" Stella cried.

"The mistress has at least six gowns to choose from," her maid said primly.

"Oooh I don't mean the mistress! I mean Miss Lucas!"

"Nothing looks good on 'er, she's so weedy, like a stick." Delia said.

"What about the expense of dressing 'er?" Stella asked. Only the Sallins' knew that money had been delivered for this purpose. "I know the mistress won't be 'appy about it, and don't be surprised, Chalamet, if you 'ave to make over some old gowns."

"Nonsense! She is too tall for any of Madame's gowns! And she cannot –

she is too thin – above." This was accompanied by a vulgar gesture.

This caused more uproarious laughter. Troy, at the landing where he had met Miss Lucas, heard it. He went up there every evening for a quiet think. He hoped she would come to him, but so far, he was out of luck. He had only been in this situation for a short time, and he was already tempted to leave it, for he would never have respect for Mr Sallins and his wife. They did not keep order, and while they did not speak disrespectfully or with vulgarity themselves, they tolerated it –

no – they even encouraged it – in the staff. He and Miss Lucas had a lot in common; neither would be happy here. He concluded however that for the moment, he would stay. Miss Lucas had nobody else in the house who had regard for her. He did not wish to leave while she was still here, he liked her.

His mistress was very kind to him. Troy was sure that if she knew of the conversations in the servants' hall she would have a word with her butler and housekeeper.

SOME TRUTHS

In the drawing room after dinner, Mrs Darcy was trying to instill some enthusiasm for a ball. She had decided to become nicer, more encouraging, and try to tell her charge what fun it would be, if only she would allow herself to have fun. She had drank several glasses of wine to put her in good humour.

"A white muslin, with a crinoline. We will engage a hair dresser to come and do an elaborate style. Your hair is good, Emily, a rich sort of chestnut, and you have to make the most of it. Now as for your skin – I want you to come with me. I have something to show you."

Emily trooped behind her as she mounted the stairs and opened the door of her boudoir. She lit the gas lamp and brought it to a room that led off the main bedroom.

It was a smaller room, but with a large mirror hanging on the wall in front of a table and chair. The room had a strong fragrance. On the table below the mirror was a jumbled assortment of bottles, pots, atomisers, jars, and sponges, brushes and rags. It looked like an artist's studio.

"You see, I am not quite a young thing anymore, no matter what you may have thought," Mrs Darcy said. "In order to retain my youthful look I have to use –

all this." Her hand swept over the melee of cosmetics under the mirror. "We shall experiment tomorrow on you, Chalamet and myself, in the day light. How old would you say I am?" she asked then, looking directly at Emily.

Emily shifted a little.

"Twenty-six?" she asked, knowing she was completely wrong, but not wishing to offend this vain woman.

"I am thirty-seven," Mrs Darcy said. "But I must swear you to secrecy on that point. People think I am much younger. However, I have a daughter aged ten."

"A daughter! Where is she?"

"She is at school. I cannot manage her here."

Emily was about to ask why, but she held her tongue.

"Of course, many people know of it," the woman went on, "But they know it should not be mentioned. I like younger men about me, and I am sure they think I am ten years younger than I really am. The trick is not to look as if I use paint, but to make it all look natural. Chalamet is very skilled. But do not misunderstand me, Emily. I like to flirt with young men, but I have no immoral intentions. I make them love me, and then I get bored, and refuse to see them, and they come to the unhappy conclusion that I am no longer in love with them."

Emily took a step backwards.

"I think it's time I went to bed," she said. "Good night, Mrs Darcy."

"Tomorrow morning after breakfast!" Mrs Darcy called after her, aggrieved that Emily had shown no enthusiasm for the pots and jars and had no reaction at all to her confession of liking young men.

COSMETICS

T he following morning saw a most unhappy Emily Lucas sitting at the table looking straight into the mirror. She could see Mrs Darcy behind her right shoulder, and Chalamet behind her left, and they were discussing her.

"How best to cover the sallowness?" Mrs Darcy frowned.

"I do not know, Madame, it is the most difficult complexion, as it shows the obvious application of pink powder. Every inch has to be completely covered, and the neck also, and in her case, it will have to go past her shoulders, for the Ball. And what of the arms? What will the lighting be like at Turkingham Hall? There is a treatment with iodide of potassium in water, and glycerine, but it must be applied daily with a sponge and whether it will do anything at all I do not know."

Emily hung her head. She felt resentful and angry.

Mrs Darcy sighed.

"I wonder if it's worth it," she said. "What is the point of trying to make her beautiful, when she will scowl in company and spoil all our work?"

"I'm not submitting to this," Emily found herself saying, getting up from the chair. She gathered her plaid skirts about her and left the room. Chalamet filed it away to tell this evening. It would be a wonderful joke!

She could not wait until dinner's end to tell her amusing story, and Troy, in the middle of his meal, had to endure it. He was silently indignant that Miss Lucas was being treated in such a way. Mrs Darcy was well-meaning, he thought, for he never thought badly of her, but she should leave Miss Lucas to be Miss Lucas.

"The cure for unhealthy, pale skin is fruit, lots of luvly apples," said the cook Mrs Jenkins. "I'm surprised the mistress doesn't know that, or you, Chalamet."

Troy filed that information away.

The following morning all fears of the ball were forgotten. Bad news came to the house.

"A telegram!" Mrs Darcy said after Sallins handed it to her on a tray. "Oh, dear, the old lady in Bristol is dead. I have to tell Miss Lucas – so find her and tell her to come in, Sallins."

Emily was walking about the back garden, the one place she was finding any peace. There was a little puppy to play with and she threw sticks for him. She came in directly, secretly fearing that she would be subjected to another attempt to make her presentable for the Ball.

"I'm sorry it's bad news," Mrs Darcy said to her. "Your great-aunt Althea is dead."

The colour left Emily's face. Mrs Darcy was surprised.

"Emily, she was old and ill," she reminded her. To herself she thought. Are we going to have hysterics? She rang the bell for a glass of wine and for her smelling salts to be brought just in case.

Emily had sunk into a chair.

"I was fond of her," she said slowly.

"Well, yes, of course you were, but there's no need for a fuss. We're too busy. We're going to choose some material for a ball gown, remember, and we cannot put it off, because Lady Ferrars is kind enough to accompany us; she has excellent taste and has got husbands for all of her nieces, whose parents thought would be on their hands forever, for they were a plain looking lot."

To herself she thought, I wonder if Mrs Loft had any money to leave? She has a son somewhere in the colonies, surely he is out of the picture now! I hope he does not return!

"I would rather not go, Cousin. I am in mourning."

"What a selfish thought! Lady Ferrars is putting herself out for us!"

"Then I beg you to go with her, and make my excuses. I don't mind what you choose."

Mrs Darcy appeared to think this was a good plan. It would be splendid not to have the dour-faced girl along with her when she was trying to impress Lady Ferrars, who had graciously offered to help find a husband for her, if nobody liked her at the Ball.

They returned home with several yards of white muslin, for which Lydia thought she had paid far too much, but Lady Ferrars had been by her side and she had to part with more of Emily's money than she had intended. She decided that she would take the bulk of the muslin for herself, and her charge? She did not need such a crinoline as was fashionable, for though she wanted her off her hands, it was unthinkable that her gown be as fine as Lydia's.

Mrs Darcy had looked forward to showing off a pretty cousin, but now she was ashamed of being seen with her. She abandoned all pretence at family feeling and began to tell everybody how burdened she was with this ill-tempered gawky girl.

THE WALK

Emily could not bear to be inside the house. Everything there was anathema to her in her present distress. As soon as Lady Ferrar's carriage had collected Cousin Lydia, she donned her cloak and slipped out the back gate into the mews. She did not want Sallins asking where she was going and when she would return. There was something about that man she did not like. A thin veneer of politeness covered his contempt. She saw it well enough though he most likely thought she was too stupid to see it. The housekeeper, Mrs Sallins, had never taken any interest in her or in her comfort. None of the maids were friendly. Knowing that she was not a favourite of their mistress, they did not trouble themselves on her behalf. Troy, only Troy had any feeling among them all.

She hurried into the mews, and immediately encountered Troy, who was tying his bootlace outside the gate.

"Miss Lucas!" he stood up. "Why are you here – can I help you?"

"I am just going for a walk, Troy."

"But why come out this way?"

She did not reply and he understood.

"It's my afternoon off and I am about to walk myself," he said. He had intended to go to Whitechapel to see his parents, but he need not set out for the East End just yet.

"Would you like to walk with me?" she immediately asked him, surprising herself that she had no shyness with him. She did not ask herself why – it was just a fact. Then it hit her – he was not judging her; he was on her side.

"Yes, I would, but not here," he said. "The windows have eyes. Let us meet at St James Church – you go there, do you not, on Sundays? I go to another, with the mistress."

She nodded and set off at a brisk pace without any more conversation. To an onlooker it would seem like a casual conversation if she were recognised.

Troy finished tying his bootlace and set off also. He wondered if she would be there or whether she had changed her mind, for a lady of the House might regret her hasty suggestion to walk with a footman. He could not see her when he reached the church, but going a little closer, he found her standing against a pillar out of sight of the passersby, and her face lit up when he appeared.

They walked down the narrow street at the side, and kept to those lanes which were not wide enough to admit carriages.

"I am sorry for your loss," he said to her.

Emily began to speak about her great-aunt and he listened.

"She rescued me from a hard situation when I was but a child," she said. She did not wish to mention the workhouse; it was shameful. "I was quite frightened of her at first, but I got used to her, and she to me, and we were a happy little family until she thought it better for me to come here to Cousin Lydia."

"Cousin Lydia – oh, that's Mrs Darcy," he said. "Are you going to go into mourning for your aunt?"

She shook her head.

"I can't. Cousin Lydia said I must not. I have one season here and –"

"And what?"

"I have to find a husband, apparently, that's their plan for me."

He was silent.

"You think you might find a man you like at the Ball?"

"I doubt I will. I don't open easily to people, and from what I heard a girl has to be a beauty and a charmer, and I'm neither."

"You are an attractive young woman," he said immediately, smiling at her.

"Troy, do not trifle with me. We are friends, are we not? I'm not like the peaches and cream girls with rosebud mouths like little dolls!"

"I don't consider them handsome," he said. "I have seen them, in my last place, where I was required to attend a few balls. The kind of beauty you describe may attract many blokes, but not me. And they may be dressed elegant, but there is very little difference between 'em all."

"Whatever do you mean?"

"They all look the same, act the same, over-anxious to impress, chattering about little or nothing, with a great deal of gossip about this person or that – I have stood near to 'em, they forget I am there, and speak freely. You are not like 'em, and please don't try to be like 'em. If they don't get a husband in one season, they're considered old, an' there's a fresh bevy of girls who will invade the next season, so the second year they're even more desperate, and the third year, they're failures. It's a cattle market. It's awful."

"How sad for them – to have to get a husband, or feel they've failed."

"I doubt there's anybody among those men for you," was his next, odd remark. He paused before he said: "That man Venables. I wouldn't trust 'im. He 'as a sly look."

"He is sly. Did you too think that I was trying to catch his attention?"

"It looked that way. Do you like 'im?"

"Not at all."

"You looked like you did like 'im, though."

"No, I overheard him say he was going to trip you up for a joke, and I took off after him, to distract him, and you passed in safety."

"What? Why would he want to do that?"

She hesitated.

"He seemed to think that my cousin favours you over his friend Mr Jennings and he wanted to humiliate you, and perhaps have you dismissed or leave, or something."

He still did not understand.

"Mr Jennings is enamoured of Mrs Darcy," he said. "What does he have to fear from me, a footman? It's all ridiculous, they must've had too much to drink."

She said nothing; he was uncomfortable with the subject, and rather annoyed, she thought.

"It was decent of you to do that," he said. "I did think it was odd you put yourself forward."

"I lost my shyness for ten seconds."

"I am glad of that." He glanced at her and smiled.

They walked on.

"To return to Venables," he said. "So you haven't set your sights on 'im. I'm glad to 'ear it. What kind of fellow do you like then, Miss Lucas?"

"A fellow who can be my friend, and taller than me with light brown eyes perhaps."

He turned toward her, mildly surprised, and then she said: "I would so like to take someone's arm, if he would like to give it."

He seemed bashful, but grinned and held out his elbow, and she slipped her arm in his. He hesitated, as if she were a mere acquaintance, before drawing it close to him.

"Do you like to be arm in arm with me?" she asked.

"Yes, I do, Miss Lucas, though it would be very much disapproved of."

"Emily."

"Emily."

"That's better."

They had wandered into a park, and never noticed which one it was, or where they were – but there was nobody about. They had so much to say to each other.

She told him that when they had guests, she found nothing to talk about, because she knew nothing, she supposed.

"You 'ave to pretend you know something. I hear 'as 'ow it's done. I once 'eard a man talk about buildings to a young lady at dinner beside him. The lady didn't know what to say, so she said 'ow much she thought a neat garden always set a nice 'ouse off, be it only a cottage, and then they 'ad a great chat about roses and he told 'er about rose windows in cathedrals and they're married now."

Emily laughed. "So if a man tells me about his shooting I'll say I love rabbit stew!"

"Something like that! But make it grouse or pheasant if 'e's a toff! Only poachers take rabbits." Then Troy changed the subject.

"You know Briggs the gardener? He 'as boxes of apples in the shed. I don't think anybody would think of telling you that you can 'elp yourself as often as you like, as long as you cover 'em up after against any frost. I 'eard," he proceeded carefully, "that fruit's good for the skin."

She stopped suddenly.

"Did you overhear talk about my skin?" she asked him, rubbing her face.

"Yes, I did." he said truthfully, hoping she would not be hurt and angry. "Though I think your skin looks very well, I don't like to think of you bein' upset about it, Chalamet has a bee in 'er bonnet about ladies complexions."

Emily had no idea that this had been discussed in the servants' hall; she concluded that he had overheard her cousin and Chalamet lamenting it when she had not been present.

"They want to put pink powder on me, I can't think of anything more objectionable, I should look like a little piglet."

"Surprise 'em, Emily! Lots of fruit! Let's go this way; there's a pear stall, I'll buy you a pear."

She did not want him to buy it for her, but he wished to and they stood in a doorstep out of public view to eat a pear each. Troy got his handkerchief and wiped pear juice from her chin and they both laughed. They stood very close together and had a moment of silence when they just looked into each other's eyes.

"May I – may I kiss you?" he asked. She nodded. It was a sweet, chaste kiss and they set out again, each feeling there was nobody else in the world.

Troy forgot to go to Whitechapel, and after walking her home as far as they dared to be seen together, he hurried away to the Mechanics Institute as was his usual habit every Tuesday because he wanted to better himself and not be in service all his life. Especially if he was going to marry a lady. He knew she had not always been a gentlewoman; the reference to 'the scullery' indicated to him that her first years had been ones of hardship. She would tell him all sometime, he was sure. She had a pure, innocent heart and he was in love with her.

TROY EXERTS INFLUENCE

T roy wrote to his parents to apologise for not going to see them. He did not give the reason. As he was going to put the letter in the post, Mr Sallins encountered him.

"Come in here, Troy," he said crisply, indicating his pantry, where they could be alone.

Troy sensed trouble and he was right. Had they been seen, he and Miss Lucas? But it was not that.

"I notice that every evening after dinner, you leave the table," Sallins complained.

Ah. He was showing them up, and Sallins did not like it.

"Why do you leave us? Are you too good for us, is that it?"

"Not at all, Mr Sallins. I'm sorry you think that, but I like to spend time alone."

"You have all the evening to be alone after your work is done," Sallins said.

"I don't like the idle chatter and the gossip, then, and the suggestive nature the conversation takes sometimes, particularly when Chalamet is on her hobby horse."

"You know, Troy, I could tell you to pack your bags and go this minute."

Troy remembered what Emily had told him. He would put it to the test.

"I would not advise that, sir."

"How dare you!"

"I would not advise it, sir. What would you say to the mistress? I think the mistress finds me agreeable."

Troy was daring him, and Sallins pursed his lips.

"You pup," he said. "You answer to me. And you stay at the table until everybody gets up to go."

"I will, if you do your part, Mr Sallins. The mistress wouldn't like to know what we talk of, and wouldn't like 'er maid to talk so freely downstairs, and about her own kin."

Sallins looked thoroughly embarrassed.

"Chalamet is a little too much," he admitted, busying himself with a pen wiper on the desk. "Very well, you may go now."

Troy turned and left the room. From that evening on, Mr Sallins exercised control over the conversation in the servants' hall. The staff was surprised and sulked a bit, and they all knew Troy had something to do with it and except for Delia they began to be careful what they said when he was around.

THE BALL

The dreaded evening arrived, the evening of the Ball.

Emily had had to sew her own gown, and as she was not an expert seamstress, it did not look as well as if a mantua-maker had given it her expert attention. It lacked the finishing touches that set a debutante apart. It had no frill, no flounce, no overskirt, and was a simple style with tight bodice and full skirt, but a skirt that could hardly earn the name of crinoline.

"No spectacles," said Cousin Lydia.

"I won't be able to see –"

"Neither will several of the debutantes. They will manage and so must you."

Thankfully there had been no more arrangements about painting her skin. She was thankful for that small mercy.

Arrayed in her new gown, her hair that had taken two hours in front of the mirror and now hurt with the amount of hairpins and combs dug into her skull, and with long white gloves to her elbows, Emily stepped carefully out of the carriage on a rainy November evening. She stepped into a puddle and splashed the gown. Fate had decided that she was not to have a good evening.

"Why can you not be more careful?" hissed her cousin. Troy was not accompanying them out, and she had no necessity to appear sweet. "Let me tell you this, Emily, you're in charge of your own fate. As soon as we enter, we shall receive dance cards. A list of dances, and a space with the name of your partner."

"How is it to be filled?" Emily asked anxiously.

"A man will approach you, I hope, and ask you for this or that dance, and you will write his name in, and make yourself available for him for that dance. I hope you are asked to dance. I will do my best for you by introducing you to all I know. And you are not to go onto the terrace with any young man, there is great danger on the terrace."

Though frightened at the thought of her first Ball, Emily felt amused at the idea that her cousin thought her in any such peril.

"Some plain girls feel that any attention paid them is to be rewarded with liberties taken – but here is Lady Ferrars and her sons, Robert and Richard. Oh! If you could catch one of those gentlemen, you would be – but it is very unlikely."

Richard was a coxcomb, an amiable chap, and Robert more serious and not at all attentive to his surroundings. Both young gentlemen disappeared after being introduced to Emily.

"Well that does it, no doubt she warned them off, for you could be seen as a gold-digger, you know, and their family has old money, though Lady Ferrars herself is of very humble origins, she had a pretty look about her, and craftiness, or so I was told, to capture a Ferrars. But you have neither."

Humble origins! Not as humble as the workhouse, Emily thought, her mind returning to the extreme deprivation and the hard labour of her childhood, the long benches full of children sitting with bowls and spoons, the cold dormitories, the harsh discipline. Is there even one person here at this Ball who was born in a workhouse? Not even the servants, she was sure, the attendants who were taking coats and cloaks. It made her feel very different, very separated from the other men and women who were making their way towards the ballroom.

She saw with embarrassment that the other young ladies had very wide crinolines. She was oddly dressed.

The crowded ballroom was a torment. It held about one hundred people, and the music, though pleasant, was designed for dancing, not listening, and the noise of chatter and laughter crushed her head like a tight helmet.

She knew nobody, she was a stranger, they were strangers, her old fears, those of isolation in a strange environment, returned with force. Her cousin was immediately engaged to dance, and left her without a thought. Emily was standing on her own, beside the chaperones and a few other girls who had not been engaged for the first dance. She drew nearer to them – would they talk to her? And make her feel welcome? But they took no notice of the girl lingering on the edge of the group. Nobody wanted to be seen with her, a tall, plain girl of no fashion.

Her head began to spin and she left the room, walked down a hallway, saw a chair and sat there for some time, looking at her blank card and wondering how it could possibly be filled when she was here, away from the dance, and loath to return to a room filled with chattering strangers who all seemed to know one another. One dance past, then another, and another and she could not bring herself to return. Then she saw two men coming toward her, though they were familiar, their approach brought no comfort. They were Jennings and Venables, no doubt sent on a mission to find her.

"Well what are you doing here? Show us your card – here, I will take the next dance, and you, Venables, the one after. Your cousin thought you were kidnapped or something. Don't be such a shy thing. We don't bite, you know."

She returned with them, and Jennings told her she was a good dancer, but said nothing more, but she felt he had danced with her simply to please Cousin Lydia. Venables was more pleasant. He seemed very curious about her. She was evasive; he smiled, but not ungently.

"It was very decent of you to intervene as you did at Mrs Darcy's house. You overheard my evil intention. I am ashamed of it now. You saw how wrong it would be. Now, Miss Lucas, it is the usual thing for couples to talk while dancing, and so I shall put to you the commonly-asked question, do you like London?"

She said nothing.

"Perhaps that is the wrong question," he said. "I understand you lived in Bristol. Did you like it there?"

"Well enough," she replied.

"And – were you born there?"

"Yes, I was."

"In what part? I know Bristol."

"In Yellowhill, Mr Venables."

"You are trifling with me," he said stiffly. "Yellowhill is a short street, it has no residences but the workhouse and affiliated buildings. You have a poor opinion of me. I will say no more."

They finished the dance. Cousin Lydia approached her as she made her way back, and taking her by the arm, drew her into a corner.

"Your behaviour tonight is abysmal! First you disappear, why? Show me your card." She took it and having glanced at it, shook her head in despair.

Emily defended herself.

"You told me you would introduce me to people, and then you went out on the floor, leaving me alone!"

"Oh you simpleton! Mr Purcell asked me to dance, and I could not refuse, for though I detest him, if you refuse the first gentleman who asks you, you cannot dance for the entire evening! You are so ignorant! Oh stop those stupid tears!" Her manner softened. "I do not know what's wrong with you. Most girls in this City would give their eye-teeth to be here, all dressed up and dancing with fine gentlemen! You would prefer to be – I do not know where you would prefer to be!"

Anywhere, anywhere with Troy, was the thought that rushed into Emily's head.

"My gown is inferior," she said. "I am ashamed of it."

"You made it yourself," was the answer. "But it appears you only learned basic dressmaking."

"I think Aunt Althea meant you to spend more on me than you are doing, Cousin Lydia. It should have been made by a dressmaker."

This was the truth, and Lydia was inwardly furious. But she took her arm, gently this time.

"Come, I will arrange some dances for you – oh! There goes Mr Halley –

where are you escaping to, Mr Halley? Slinking off to the card room? But here is a charming young lady in need of a partner! You will not refuse her, it is her very first Ball!"

The middle-aged man stopped, looked rather confused, bowed, and asked her for a dance. When that was over, he asked her for a second before he resumed his steps to the card room.

"You have made an impression, perhaps a conquest," smiled Cousin Lydia. "He is a bachelor! And very rich."

In the old adage that nothing succeeds like success, Emily was not without a partner for the rest of the evening, for some older married men were prodded in her direction by their wives, who were tired of dancing and did not want their husbands to dance with any young popular beauty, for some debutantes had already drawn the eyes of many admiring men like bees to a flower. Other wives had been watching her in an idle way and taken pity on her and sent their husbands over.

It was a perfectly wretched time, and she was exhausted and very glad to sit in the carriage to go home. Cousin Lydia was quiet. Her mind was busy, and a confusion of thoughts and feelings. Firstly, was that she had not enjoyed herself, and Emily had had nothing to do with that. Every gentleman there had filled her, Lydia, with distaste. Her head was in her own home, with a young man who was most likely chatting with the maids in the servants' hall, a tall, handsome young man who whenever he drew near to her made her feel a little light-headed. Her footman, James Troy. He would forever serve her, she would make it happen such. He would never leave her house. She must make his position very attractive for him to remain in, with greater renumeration and the promise of promotion.

When Emily came downstairs the following morning, her heart was flooded with consolation when she espied Troy in the hall. Perhaps he was there deliberately to meet her? Her cousin was not down yet, so they took a risk of speaking together. He straightened a picture on the wall.

"How was it?" he asked her, as she needlessly rearranged a flower in a vase.

"Awful. Just awful."

"Surely not that bad, not every man in Town is awful!"

"The only one who is not, was not there. But it wasn't just that, it was a lot more."

They did not dare speak for longer, and Emily passed into the breakfast room. Troy was present at breakfast, busying himself around the buffet, and Lydia was her usual pleasant self to her young cousin when he was in attendance.

"Are you very fatigued, dear? You will have to get used to the attention, you know. I have decided I am giving a dance for you, here in this house!"

Emily looked up suddenly with bright eyes; she'd have Troy within her sight all night long, the possibilities were pleasant to think of.

"You are looking forward to it?" asked Lydia, but she looked a little bewildered.

"I won't ruin my gown stepping into a puddle," Emily said hurriedly. "I really did get off to a bad beginning last evening!"

"Oh, was that it? That's why you ran down the passage, and I had to send two gentlemen after you to bring you back! Troy!" She addressed him, somewhat flirtatiously, Emily thought. "Troy, Miss Lucas had so many admirers last evening that I predict she will be married before Easter!"

"But you forget something important, Cousin," she interjected. "How many did I like? Not one!"

Silence met this. After Troy had taken the dishes away, Cousin Lydia leaned toward her.

"You will have to be engaged before the end of January," she said. "I do not believe that none of the men there last night pleased you. There are widowers. At least three last evening. Some have motherless children. It would be a fine, very noble thing to marry a widower with children. I always think that children deprived of their mothers suffer great loneliness. My poor Daphne writes to me of hers."

"Widowers? Are they not too old for me? What of bachelors?"

Lydia dabbed her lips with her napkin.

"I suppose there is Mr Jennings," she said. "And Mr Purcell." She bit her lip.

Emily gave a silent smile. Those men were Lydia's rejects.

"What of Mr Venables?" she ventured. "I thought perhaps he liked me a little bit, but you said he was unavailable to me."

"Mr Venables? Likes you –?" This was said with incredulity, and Emily did not expand the subject.

THE GREEN-EYED MONSTER

The dance was to take place just before Christmas. But late in November, bad news came to the house from France. Chalamet's mother died unexpectedly.

She did not return to France, instead she bore her sorrow away from her family. Emily made her a sympathy card, and wrote it all in French using a calligraphy pen and coloured inks. She took a piece of silver cord from the workbasket and sewed it on the edges.

Chalamet was very surprised to receive it, and very touched. She turned it over in her hands.

"You are very kind, Miss Lucas," she said, with tears in her eyes. "I will not forget your good heart." She went away, looking at the card made with tenderness and regard, and repented of all her unkind mockery of Miss Lucas when she had first arrived in Cavendish Square. Her mistress was not so kind, and gave impatient sighs when tears came into her eyes at unexpected moments.

"She has no control over her feelings," she complained to Emily one day. "She should be getting over this. Red eyes are affecting her looks, and I can't bear to have unpleasant looking people about me. By the way, your skin has improved. What are you doing?"

"I'm eating fruit and getting fresh air," Emily said. "When will Daphne come?" she asked, changing the subject. She was looking forward to having a child in the house, she liked children, and it would remove the attention that oppressed her.

"Oh, Daphne is not coming." Cousin Lydia said, flicking the pages of *The Gentlewoman*. "It's too boring for her here, with no other children about. She far prefers to go with her friends and their parents to France for Christmas. To a chateau, no less!"

"Surely she should come and spend it with her own mother!" Emily burst out.

"Oh, no, I do not signify much in her life. She looks on Mr and Mrs Allcott as her mother and father by now, I should think."

Emily's heart went out to the little girl. Every three or four days a letter arrived from Daphne to her mother. A letter set aside and forgotten after being quickly read. Emily had never heard her cousin refer to having to write to Daphne, or that she must tell Daphne this or that, nor were any parcels or gifts sent to the child. It seemed like the cruelest neglect. But she said nothing.

"Now for the dance!" Lydia was in her element as she threw the magazine aside. The drawing room and the dining room were not very large, but there was a wide connecting door which she had thrown open. "We have enough space for twenty couples to dance easily about the drawing room, and we shall move the cabinet from that corner and put the orchestra there. The supper room can be set out across the hall in the green parlour, and cards can go on in the study."

"Cards!"

"Yes, for I won't get gentlemen to come without the promise of a card table. Gentlemen don't like dances, as a rule. Mr Halley, I know, never attends anything without cards. Do you play cards, Emily?"

"No, not at all. Aunt Althea disapproved of them."

Her cousin sighed.

"I haven't time to teach you," she said. "Mr Halley might like it if you could play a game of whist."

"Mr Halley!"

"Or Mr Jennings or anybody." She fell silent, for they heard Delia come into the connecting room from the hall, humming as was her fashion. It was her time to dust there. She ceased humming and began to speak to somebody else who had just come in behind her, also from the hall.

Unaware that her mistress and Miss Lucas were nearby, she teased the newcomer.

"You followin' me, Troy? I was in the green parlour, and you come in, and now I come 'ere, and you come in 'ere too! If I didn't know any better I'd say you was sweet on me! But I only like Durham lads."

"Durham lads for Durham lasses, then." Troy replied cheerfully as they heard the clock being wound.

"Oh I wouldn't be as strict as all tha', I might, just might, walk out wi' a Cockney if he was smart an' nice."

"I 'ave a friend a Cockney, a nice bloke, you might like 'im."

"Aren't you a Cockney, Troy?"

"Well, there's the clock wound up." They heard him leave the room.

Cousin Lydia's expression had turned stony.

Poor Delia! Emily waited for the axe to fall, but nothing happened, though when Delia came through the connecting door a few minutes later, she seemed discomfited to find them there.

The following morning the housekeeper came as usual to the dining room to receive her orders for the day. She was just about to go to the kitchen again when Mrs Darcy asked her to remain for a moment.

"Mrs Sallins, the maid Delia. How is her work?"

"It's very good, Madam, I have no complaint."

"I'm not satisfied, Mrs Sallins. After she dusted yesterday I found an area of the sideboard which had crumbs on it."

Mrs Sallins was silent. Emily looked at Lydia with astonishment.

"I will speak to her, Madam."

"I also have some questions about her character. It has come to my notice that she flirts."

"I was not aware of that, Madam." Mrs Sallins lied. She knew that Delia was enamoured of Troy. She was a girl, after all, and Troy was handsome. Of course she flirted. What maids did not flirt with the footmen?

"I wish you to dismiss her, Mrs Sallins."

"Madam, I –"

"I will brook no argument! Give her two weeks wages now and put her out. And – I wish you to give the other maids a good talking to — about decorum and going about their work in silence. And when interviewing maids in future, I think it would be better to engage plain, older women, rather than young pretty ones. Not too old though, they have to be able to work hard."

Mrs Sallins took a deep breath before she said: "Yes, Madam," and left the room.

Emily could hardly believe that poor Delia had been dismissed because Cousin Lydia had suspected a rival for her affections. And the lie about the crumbs! Delia would be gone in an hour, and nobody downstairs would know the particulars. It was a very unfair world. She knew the same fate awaited her if Lydia found out that she and Troy were meeting regularly.

"You are very quiet, Emily. When you have an establishment of your own, you will also have to deal with this unpleasantness. But as to getting your own establishment, you seem disinterested. It must be nice for you to live here and to have somebody else responsible for all that. It will not last forever, you know. Easter, and you'll have your own house, and staff. But you need to work harder! I'm going to all this trouble for you, and I don't think you appreciate it at all."

Downstairs, Mrs Sallins had rushed to her husband who was inspecting the plates in the pantry. He heard her, astonished.

"She must have heard her talk to Troy."

"And I have to engage a plain old maid to replace her."

"This will become a very dull house, unless the new maid falls in love with me."

"Why isn't the mistress in love with you? I would willingly give you up for a few treasures, for rich women in love with poor men shower them with expensive gifts."

"Alas, no such luck. That is the footman's fate, not mine."

"She is more infatuated with him every day. He does not even see it. Yesterday she asked him about his family, and even suggested he bring his mother to meet her someday!"

THE SECRET

Troy and Emily met every night for a few minutes after the household had gone to bed. She exited her room with a candle and stole quietly to the end of the passage, and he came down from his attic room. There was a small side passage beside the servant's stairwell, a dark and crooked little place that led to a large closet for bric-a-brac. It was used also as a sleeping place for the cook's cat, who got in a narrow window after she was put outside every evening and settled in a corner on an old rug. It was above the study and that was locked at night. Here, in this cold place, with the narrow window overlooking the alley, they whispered and embraced before parting again to return to their chambers. Meeting outside was more difficult. Troy's work day began at six-thirty and he was not free to retire until nine. However, he was allowed some freedom in the afternoon between lunch and laying the table for dinner.

Emily was glad to leave the house in the afternoons. Lydia objected first to her request to be allowed to leave the house on her own for a walk, and accused her of trying to get out of work, for it was her responsibility now to make and mend all her clothes. The money that had been given to Lydia for her was apparently now set aside for her 'when she married'.

"If I don't get a walk, I get a headache," Emily had said. It was not a lie, the moment she stepped out from the house she felt her head clearing as if she were leaving her anxieties and tensions behind. London had long since lost the bad smells of the hot months, and though there was fog, it was bracing, and in certain places by the river Thames, the thick air from coal fires was lessened, depending on the wind.

The sweethearts had to vary their meeting places and it had to be far enough from Cavendish Square so as not to be seen by any neighbours.

One day, he was a little quiet and Emily asked him what the matter was.

"You and me," he replied somewhat reluctantly. "You're far above me, and tell me if you're just toying with me, for it's widely believed you are getting married to some rich old fellow soon."

"Troy, Troy! Firstly, I'm not far above me. I am very much below you." She sighed. She was afraid of his reaction when she told him that she had been born in the workhouse, and worse than that – her mother and father had been unwed.

He was a little shocked.

"Nobody knows. Cousin Lydia doesn't know. Oh Troy, are you very upset about it? Will it make a difference to us?"

"No difference to us," Troy said, squeezing her hand hard. "You had a hard start in life then. You're the daughter of a gentleman and a maid. Your poor mother. He should've married her, he must be a cad."

"I suppose he is," she said sadly. "He doesn't acknowledge me at all."

They walked on.

"And – you're not going to marry some rich old fellow?"

"No, I am not."

He turned toward her and the thin sun lit up his face. He looked abashed but hopeful.

"Will you marry a poor young fellow then?"

"Yes, I will, if he's you."

Joy filled them and they walked on, entwined, until it was time to go home. How they would marry, and upon what they would live, was as yet uncertain. They pledged themselves to each other in secret for now.

SCANDAL

The sweethearts did not spend much time together in the weeks before Christmas. Mrs Darcy engaged Troy to her completely in the afternoons as she wished to shop, and he went in the carriage, sitting on the box alongside the coachman until their destination was reached.

"I daresay you will miss your walk if you come with me," Lydia said to Emily when the latter suggested that she would like to come on a shopping expedition. But Lydia did not want her with her.

These trips were an imposition on Troy as he no longer had afternoons to himself, but that did not occur to Lydia. Troy only existed for her use, and she never thought that he might have things to do for himself. Servants' hours were not set. They were available to their masters or mistresses all the hours of the day if the latter chose.

Mrs Darcy thought she was doing Troy a great favour by taking him to the posh shops on Bond St. She summoned him to go in with her, and asked his opinion on items she liked. He was vague; he had no preference for a bronze candlestick or a silver for her friends or a Wedgewood or a Dresden for Lady Ferrars. When she made her choice, he carried the purchases to the carriage.

"I have high hopes for you, Troy," she said to him, smiling. "I have long thought that I need a personal aide. You would no longer wear the uniform; instead you would outfit yourself as a clerk. It would be a step up for you. Now I want to get a present for your mother. Would she like a nice warm muffler? This Kashmiri wool is particularly fine!"

Troy was quietly very pleased to hear that promotion was in the offing – he had to earn as much as he could to keep a wife.

"I hope this ceases after Christmas," Emily whispered to him as they stood together in the little crooked hallway that night. "I think she likes you too much, more than a mistress should like a servant."

"No, not you too," he groaned. "My friends all say the same thing. She 'as no wishes of that kind, the kind you imply. I'm glad you told me her age, cos I know she can't be interested in me if she's that old. I'm just a servant boy. I'm from Whitechapel, the East End! I'm nobody; my father was in service, and my mother too, we are humble people. Above all, I'm taken." He kissed her lightly.

"But she doesn't know that! She wants to meet them, doesn't she?"

"Well yes, but that isn't unusual, for an employer to want to meet the family of a servant. It's a mark of approval, I grant you that but it doesn't mean anythin' at all. Come now, let's stop talking of her. I've 'ad her all day long; I've been bored to tears standin' around shops bein' asked my opinion on everything and I've been thinkin' about kissin' you this long time."

Emily felt herself happy and at peace when she was in his arms. They struggled with keeping their embraces chaste; they wished more than anything to be one with each other.

"She's a good chaperone," Troy said, indicating the cat, who never slept when they were there, but sat on her little mat and stared at them like the strictest of duennas, her eyes two amber points in the shadows.

"I just think she wishes us gone, and is trying to intimidate us," giggled Emily. "But it's time for us to go anyway, so Persia gets her way, doesn't she?"

"She's not even a Persian cat, she only thinks she is," Troy said. "And so does Mrs Jenkins. Goodnight, turtledove."

Persia was able to get in because Mrs Jenkins left the little window open for her. The couple closed the window while they were there, and Troy reopened it when leaving so that Persia could get out again in the morning and make her way by whatever means to the kitchen door where she would be fed. One day, he forgot to open the window, and Persia was seen walking majestically down the main staircase at breakfast time. She was spotted by Mrs Darcy.

"Why is Mrs Jenkins' cat in here?"

"She must've slipped in the back door earlier and gone upstairs," Emily said quickly. She saw Troy out of the corner of her eye behind Mrs Darcy, dashing the palm of his hand against his forehead, and could barely keep from laughing.

"Troy!"

"Yes, Madam." He came, his countenance serious.

"Take this cat out and tell Mrs Jenkins that if I ever find her in here again I will be very angry."

Poor Mrs Jenkins did not know how this incursion had happened, and Troy had to tell her that he had seen the window open on his way to bed and had shut it, but reassured her that he would not shut it in the future.

"I will keep your secret," he said solemnly. "Madam does not know she got in that way. Don't worry, Mrs Jenkins. Oh, she's calling me," he sped off to the first of many calls that day. She wished to go shopping in the afternoon.

They were in a crowded shop later and were seen from a distance by two of her friends who had met accidentally and had stopped to chat.

"Oh look, there's Mrs Darcy!" Mrs Howard said in a whisper.

"I thought she was not going to shop today," said Mrs Glover with some indignation. "I asked her to come with me to choose silver for my new daughter-in-law, and she said that she had business at home. Look at her now! She's with that good-looking footman!"

"Again! She takes him everywhere with her now!"

"To carry her purchases?"

"He does not have to come into the shop and accompany her everywhere, he can be sent for, when needed. As I do with mine. He is outside the front door, and the shop boy takes the boxes down, and Norris fetches the coach and brings it around and puts them in. That's what everybody does. No, there is something more here, Eleanor. She is seen too much with him."

"Beatrice! You are not saying – she would be shunned by all respectable people. His station in life is so low!"

"I say she is mad with love, and I am not the only one to say that, Eleanor."

"Someone should speak to her!"

"Who? Who dares? We are to go to this dance for her protegée, Miss Lucas, and we can perhaps find out a little more about the whole thing."

"It would be preposterous! She would be dropped by everybody!"

"Let us walk past her very deliberately without acknowledging her to let her know what we think of her behaviour. I will cut her when she's with that footman."

THE WALTZ

For Mrs Darcy, the dilemma was real. She was in love with Troy. She was still a handsome woman – and she need never reveal her true age to him. Her daughter could become her 'orphaned ward'. But they could not marry and live in England – not in England! They would never be accepted here. On the continent however, many irregular marriages were tolerated. The thousand pounds was largely intact. She had only spent fifty on Emily. The dance would cost money –

it was to be regretted, but she could not back away. Hopefully there would be no further expenses. She still had her own inheritance from her husband. It was banked and she lived off the interest quite well, as most wealthy people did.

It never occurred to her that Troy might not be in love with her or might have plans of his own for his life. All the advantage of a match with her was in *his* favour. He would live as a gentleman. She would make him a generous allowance and his parents could move out of the East End to a more respectable area so that she could visit them. She could not have relations in the East End.

The dance was to take place on the Saturday before Christmas, and all became ready.

"I must say you have very much improved in looks," Lydia commented to her cousin. "The fruits, as you mentioned, though Mrs Jenkins will complain about the apples running out early. You have also filled out a bit and are not so rakish. You smile sometimes, I see you smile to yourself. Have you got a secret? If it is a man, I demand to know."

She received no answer, which annoyed her greatly. *'The mark of a happy heart is a cheerful face,'* she muttered to herself. She had heard it somewhere a long time ago.

Emily's walk took her one day to a little jeweller's shop where she bought a gold heart-shaped locket, and she put a little miniature of herself in it. She had sat one afternoon for an artist whose studio she had often passed.

"You are to be particularly attentive to Mr Halley tonight," Cousin Lydia said to her on the day of the dance. "He is becoming attached to you. If he proposes, you are to accept."

"Why would he propose, Cousin? Beyond dancing with me twice, he has shown no interest." Emily said.

"If he has not, it's because you rebuffed him. You are such trouble to me! I wish you had never come here!"

The house was in a flurry to get everything ready, but by the time the musicians arrived it was ready and Emily was dressed.

"You look so lovely, Miss Lucas," Chalamet gushed. "You have elegance!" Chalamet was now firmly on her side.

"Thank you, Chalamet." The afternoons with nothing to do after her walks –

short as many were – because of inclement weather – had improved her dressmaking skills. Her gown tonight was far superior to the one she had worn for the Ball. It was not new; she had asked Lydia for one that she could make over. Pleased to be spared expense, Lydia parted with a ruby tulle gown and a pale pink velvet spencer jacket. Emily had picked both apart. She made the tulle into an overskirt for her white muslin, with pink velvet bows and pink velvet worked into the sleeves and bodice to create a frilly, floaty effect. There was a slight train. Chalamet, who had a flair for design, helped her enormously and gave her a crinoline cage belonging to her mistress. Lydia had not taken much notice of her preparations; her mind was elsewhere.

Emily was able to dress herself on the evening of the dance, and only needed a little help with her stays, the buttons at the back of her gown and the arrangement of her hair in curls piled on her head, and Chalamet had worked miracles with a length of tulle and a few combs for her head.

"Miss Emily, if we pull a few little curly tendrils of your hair down each side of your face, they will enhance your look, and give strength to your little chin. There!"

Emily could hear the musicians and tripped downstairs on her own, hoping to see Troy before she saw anybody else. She was in luck – he was in the drawing room on a stepladder lighting the candles –for tonight this was to be the ballroom, and he was in his dress livery – royal blue and white – and when he saw her his eyes lit with admiration.

"Do I look all right?" she asked eagerly, twirling about, sending the scent of her violet perfume in all directions as she turned.

"You look beautiful," he said. The musicians were tuning their instruments. The room was dimly lit as yet, and the only other figure there besides the musicians was the Duke of Wellington looking on them from his portrait.

"Play a Strauss waltz," she told the musicians impulsively. She hurried to the doors and shut them. He climbed down and put the taper away. She swept back to her sweetheart, and placed her left hand on his right upper arm. He drew her to him and encircled her waist with his hand. The other hands were clasped outstretched and the music began –a smooth harmony, a medley of beautiful, young romantic sound.

He led her around the candlelit room for as long as the waltz lasted – about five minutes. They were in their own world, looking at each other with tender longing and feelings too deep and happy for words, they did not need to talk. Then it ended – too soon – reality returned. Troy had to tend to the chandeliers, she to go upstairs again to descend with her cousin as if she were making her first entrance.

Lydia was astonished that the young woman she had thought a donkey looked so attractive. Her complexion was bright and cheeks rosy. She seemed a little out of breath and her eyes sparkled. She felt pleased at first, then a little jealous. Emily would be preferred over her tonight. Emily glowed with youth. It was untenable.

As the guests arrived, Emily greeted them with sincere smiles. I wonder how I feel so much at ease and happy, she asked herself. It's because I am in love! My heart is happy, and I radiate it! She was popular, sought after, though not at all vivacious or flirty. Her serenity and her new appreciation of people around her moved her mind from herself. She was hostess and her guests should feel comfortable and happy.

PROSPECT OF PROMOTION

Cousin Lydia was not at all as popular as she wished to be. She was cross, and this heaviness showing in her countenance, no matter how much she tried to smile, turned the fickle socialites, men and women, away. She had seen the two ladies cut her very deliberately the other day. They were here tonight and beyond a courteous nod, they had avoided her. In her own house!

"You have worked a miracle with Miss Lucas," Ashton Venables said to her.

This put her in a bad temper. Venables was a man who had always been around her when she needed him, but she was in the habit of pushing him away. At one time she might have settled for Mr Venables, but now there was Troy. Only Troy.

She sought refuge in her footman. Troy was standing by the door with a tray of champagne glasses. She went to him and helped herself to one. He had been watching his love in admiration. He was happy that she was at ease, and did not feel at all jealous or threatened by the attention she was receiving from the young men present. Occasionally their eyes met in a secret look. It was risky, but they could not help themselves – her mind and heart was with him, and his with her. Now he had to tear himself away to pay attention to his mistress.

"I am weary of all this, Troy," she was saying. "It is such a shallow, empty life. I long to go away. To be abroad."

"The weather would be better abroad, Madam."

"Oh I do not care about the weather. I want a quiet domestic life. I shall go to Switzerland in the spring, I think. But I must take a servant, and I will need a personal secretary, an assistant, for I have so many matters of business, I cannot keep up. What say you, Troy? Will you take the promotion? We would go for six weeks. I will take Chalamet, she might like to go and visit her family in France. You would be an upper servant, if indeed you could be called a servant at all. I will triple your wages. Switzerland is such a stunning place – the mountains, the snow. Think about it, Troy. Promotion – if you come with me. Only six weeks."

Troy was astounded with this offer. He mumbled something in thanks, and his mistress drew away.

Mr Halley did not turn up for the dance. Lydia supposed that he had hit the bottle again. He had a reputation for overdoing spirits, for disappearing from society for weeks at a time. It was hopeless. How could she rid herself of Emily before she left for Switzerland? She was not going to take her with them. Mr Hally would be made to propose to her, and she would be made to accept him.

Emily's dance card was full. Mr Venables danced the first two dances with her which was regarded as a mark of attachment.

"Tell me again where you were born," he asked her.

"I was born at Yellowhill, Bristol."

"You intrigue me," he said. "I do not know if you are playing with me. Are you?"

"I do not play, sir." Emily could see Troy behind him. She hoped that nobody noticed the glare he directed toward Venables' back. Later in the night, Venables grew angry when the footman overfilled his wine glass causing it to overflow onto his hands and starched cuffs. "I beg your pardon, sir," said Troy, pulling out his handkerchief and making a show of wiping off the red stains. "I shall procure you another glass directly," and went away and did not return.

The sweethearts met again that night. Emily carried a little box with her.

"Merry Christmas," she whispered. He smiled when he saw her gift. She put it around his neck and kissed him.

"I have something for you," he said a little awkwardly. He took a ring from his pocket and placed it on her finger.

"It's not as fine as I would wish –"

"It's beautiful, darling!"

"But I am getting promotion soon – so that will help us, I shall be in service no longer, but be a clerk."

He told her about Mrs Darcy's plans to take him abroad. Her expression altered from delight to concern.

"She is taking you away from me," she said simply.

"Surely you are to come too!"

She shook her head. "I doubt very much she means me to go."

"It's only for six weeks, turtledove."

"I am not sure, Troy. I don't trust her."

"Let's not spoil our evening." He kissed her. "We'll talk about it tomorrow."

"I loved the dance with you. Where did you learn to dance, Troy?"

"In little Whitechapel parlours, small as they are, everybody learns to dance!"

RAGE

I t was quite a job to put the house to rights the
following day, and Troy was a little careless. He was
moving furniture back to their proper places when
Mrs Darcy entered the drawing room. Somebody had left
a fan on a chair which fell to the floor. He leaned down to
retrieve it, and as he did the heart-shaped locket escaped
it's hiding place under his shirt collar and swung into
sight.

"Oh Troy! What a lovely little object!" Mrs Darcy
exclaimed.

"Oh, yes, Madam." He stuffed it in under his collar again.

"Was that a Christmas gift Troy?" her voice was cloying,
flirty.

He just smiled, blushed deeply and said "Yes, Madam", and
she felt affronted. It was a gift. And her footman would not

tell her anything about it! Who gave a locket to another? A close family member or a sweetheart! If his mother had given it to him, he would have said so, there was nothing to hide, nothing to blush about. *I got it from my mother, Madam.'* Nothing embarrassing in that. The blush gave him away.

She felt angry. Troy had a lover? The possibility had never entered her head before. He was a very busy footman, he went to Whitechapel only every two months, and he had received this gift in the last twenty-four hours. Somebody had given it to him last night? Not another maid? Who? Stella, not Stella. She was walking out with a servant from another house. Not Prue, the middle-aged maid engaged to replace Delia. Not Chalamet! Chalamet was above him, very much above a footman. She trembled with rage, jealousy and a burning to know who his sweetheart was.

She called for her carriage and went to her lawyer, who gave her the name of a retired metropolitan policeman who did private work. She went to his house there and then, and engaged him for the following day.

"You have worked so hard of late, Troy," she said casually. "I have no need of you for the next few afternoons. Tell Sallins I said you are to be free."

"Thank you, Madam!" Was it her imagination, or was he elated? She felt aggrieved. Surely he would miss going out with her for the afternoon, shopping? But no, he was not at all disappointed.

When Emily unwrapped her napkin at lunch, she found a note. '*3pm, Circus. Love, T.*' She deftly moved the napkin to her lap with the note still in it, and slipped the note into her pocket. She was adept at this by now and nothing was ever suspected.

"The weather has cleared, I shall walk this afternoon," she told her cousin, who just shrugged.

It was late that evening when Lydia had a visitor. She saw him in the drawing room and Emily was present, so she told her to leave the room.

"Here's what I found, Madam," said the old policeman. "As there are two doors in this house, I put a man on the back gate. I myself saw a lady leave the house around two thirty."

"Yes, that would be my cousin."

"Yes, the one I just saw now in the room."

"Meantime, my man, he sees the tall footman leave by the back gate and he follows him."

"Yes, yes?"

"And he goes to Piccadilly Circus, and he meets someone there. A lady."

"Certainly not a lady, a servant girl I suppose."

"A lady, Madam, in a green coat, the same as I saw leaving the house. Tall, spectacles, green bonnet with red ribbon, green coat."

Mrs Darcy sat down weakly.

"I do not believe it," she said. "It can't be her."

"Would you like me to follow them again, Madam?"

"No, the information is very useful to me."

"If that is all, Madam, I will take my leave then and send you the bill."

He made an exit, telling Troy to get his mistress a cup of tea for she'd had some kind of shock. He put on his hat and left.

Emily. She did not believe it. There had been some mistake. She would follow Emily herself on the morrow.

So she did. This time the venue was a little street off Hanover Square, and she saw them meet and embrace and walk away hand in hand. *Troy and Emily!*

Rage consumed her – a deep, jealous rage. Emily would not have him! Never! Shaking, she went home and went to bed early and had her dinner sent up with orders she was not to be disturbed. She could not face Emily. She felt that she was quite capable of killing the girl.

After some hours, her rage subsided, her mind cleared, and she came to some conclusions.

She still wanted Troy for herself.

She wanted Emily married to Mr Halley.

She did not want Troy to know that she hated Emily. She must feign affection for her, for jealousy was not an attractive trait.

She had to get Troy quickly away. It was not possible now to wait for spring – they had to leave England very soon.

She had to behave normally, if that were possible.

I WILL NOT MARRY!

Mrs Darcy looked with distaste at the neglected house in this now unfashionable part of London. Mr Halley had let it go. It looked as if nobody had lived in it for years. And as he spent most of his time at his club, it was probably true that it was almost uninhabited.

He was from the North of England; it was said that he had a castle there. An old pile that belonged in Jacobean times, freezing cold. He did not spend winters there, but used his house in Town, this unappealing house.

She knocked on the door and heard a shuffling to the door. An ancient retainer pulled it open with a creak. He wore an old-fashioned suit that was wrinkled and too large for him. No doubt it had fit him as a younger man. He wore a ruffled shirt as if he belonged in the last century.

She was shown to a musty, cold drawing room. The aged retainer apologised for the lack of a fire, but 'the Master' never used this room; he liked his study better. He pulled the curtains back and Mrs Darcy sneezed in a shower of dust.

She declined refreshment, sure that the tea would be stale and the cups stained. What a dreadful place this was.

He came down in ten minutes.

"Mrs Darcy! To what do I owe the honour?"

"I have been meaning to see you for some time, Mr Halley," she lied. "My late husband was your friend, and I should not neglect you."

"Ah, such a good man!"

They reminisced about the late gentleman for a time, until Mrs Darcy decided it was time to come to the point.

"My young cousin," she said. "Miss Emily Lucas. You seemed a little taken with her at the Ball."

"She is a pleasant, unspoiled girl, pretty I thought, though not in a conventional way."

"She is in the market for a husband, Mr Halley."

"Well I hope you are not thinking of me for her – I'm over forty! What would she want with an old man like me?"

"Do not do yourself down so! You are not old. She likes you. She is quite in love with you. She was so disappointed you did not appear at our dance, as I was! She looked stunning and gathered quite a few admirers around her, all dying for a smile to be thrown their way, but she would not be consoled, for you were not there. Were you to propose, I am very confident that you would not be refused."

"Oh, come now, I am flattered – but I am set in my ways – an old bachelor like me – I have no inclination to marry, really."

"Oh but you must, Mr Halley. Who will you leave all your money to? Would you not like an heir or two? It is not too late!"

He hemmed and hawed, clasped and unclasped his hands, and finally said:

"No, for I would not be a good husband to any woman. I know my faults."

"But it would be the role of your wife to help you with those faults! Just think how sweet it would be, Mr Halley! She is dying for love of you!"

"I do not believe you."

"She is very shy and diffident, and easily embarrassed. Such a sensitive, modest nature! Should you change your mind, I have a plan..." She talked on, and he kept shaking his head.

"But will you think on it?" she appealed to him.

"I will think on it," he lied, to get rid of her.

As soon as she got home, she pulled off her gloves and asked for Emily to be sent to the drawing room directly.

"Cousin Lydia, is there something the matter?" Emily was alarmed, Lydia's behaviour had been very odd of late. She had been on edge and had hardly spoken to her, but avoided her, taking her meals in her room, pleading illness and emphasising that she wished to see nobody at all, not even her young cousin.

"Sit down, Emily. The time has come."

"For what?"

"For you to marry Mr Halley."

"I'm not going to marry Mr Halley."

"You are, you stubborn girl! That is why you were sent here, to marry well! I have just seen him, and he is willing to have you."

Emily got up abruptly.

"I am not going to marry him. You cannot force me up the aisle. I will say 'no' at the altar; instead of 'I do' I will say: I do not. It's wrong of you to make me marry! My late aunt provided me with enough money and I would like that given to me to make my own way, please."

Lydia was stunned. Emily had developed a bold impudence, a disgusting defiance, what had altered her? Gone was the timidity. She knew the reason well. She thought she had James Troy in her pocket. She would get an ugly surprise before long.

"I am going abroad soon. You are not coming with me. Leave me. I do not want to see you." Emily needed no encouragement, she left the room, leaving her cousin fuming. She would marry Mr Halley, she could force her to do so. And she knew she could.

She summoned Troy next, and swapped her nasty side for her sweet, kind side.

"Well Troy, have you thought about accompanying me abroad as my assistant? I wish to know, as my plans may escalate very soon. I find we will have to leave much sooner than expected."

"I would be honoured, Madam." Troy bent his head. The sunlight caught his brown-gold hair and she longed to put her hand on it. But there would be time for that. She, Lydia, would be Mrs Troy in the Spring, married in a little mountain chapel at the foot of the Alps, and settling perhaps in Italy.

"That gives me happiness and ease, Troy. I am uncommonly fond of all the members of my household, and it will give me pleasure to travel with you and Chalamet, for I think of you both as my friends, rather than my servants."

Troy had a suspicion for the first time that she was more interested in him than appropriate, but he let it go. He wondered if it would be a good time to tell her that he was engaged to be married. But she could be angry – a servant was supposed to ask permission to become engaged. It was so in many houses. The personal lives of the servants was the business of the people they served. He had better say nothing.

"Is there – is there anybody else to accompany us, Madam?"

"No, indeed not. Mr and Mrs Sallins will stay as caretakers while I am away. We will have to turn out the others, unfortunately. No doubt you wonder about Miss Lucas? She will not come. She has duties and obligations that she may not renege on."

It was not appropriate for Troy to ask what arrangements she had made for Miss Lucas, and so he kept his mouth shut.

"We will leave in one week, Troy. And do take me to meet your mother and father first! For I wish to tell them that they have raised a fine young man, with good prospects, which I will do my best to advance. What about in three days time? We shall go there on Friday afternoon."

Troy walked back to his duties, his mind full of thoughts and questions. He still did not believe that Mrs Darcy had any personal interest in him. She was a kind lady who wished to see him advance. Now he had to write to his mother directly; the little house would have to be made ready for an important guest.

WORKHOUSE REVEAL

The sweethearts met that evening and had a desperate conversation in whispers in the old passageway.

"Troy – do not go with her to Europe! She doesn't intend to return!"

"Did she say that?"

"No, but –"

"– I must go, turtledove. We can't get married without mint."

"She's taking my money, I know I'll never see it. It is so wrong of her!"

"Oh she will give it back, I'm sure she will, someday, she just thinks you're not old enough to manage it. Perhaps she'll pay some friends to put you up while we're gone."

"Oh Troy, you think too well of everybody! She wants to force me to marry!"

"Shhh!" he put his fingers over her lips. "You'll wake the 'ouse."

"She wants me to marry that Mr Halley. She'll contrive some trick. Duties and obligations! I know what she means!"

"Nobody can trick someone into marrying someone."

"No? I've heard of opium being given, and clergymen duped or bribed."

"I 'ave an idea – you can stay with my people in Whitechapel. We're responsible for you now!"

"That's a good idea." But her old fears came back to her – strange place, strange people! But if they were Troy's parents, they must be good people! Good and welcoming, like him.

"I keep wonderin' if I oughter tell Madam we're engaged." Troy said. "But then, she saw the locket – an' remarked it, so she knows I 'ave a sweetheart. Why would she 'ave designs on me, when she knows I 'ave a sweetheart?"

"At least she doesn't know it's me," Emily said, totally unaware that she was very wrong indeed.

"I 'ave a locket for you too, I got my likeness done the same place as you." Troy took the chain and oval-shaped case from his inside pocket and put it into her hand.

"I will treasure this," Emily said happily.

Mrs Darcy thought that as the house was being shut up that Emily would panic and fret and worry about where she was to go. But she went about blithely.

"You must help me," complained her cousin. "I'm up to my eyes trying to make everything ready, and you're swanning about without a care in the world. I can't think why. Where will you go?"

"There's always the workhouse," Emily said.

"You impudent, ungrateful brat!"

"I'm not a stranger to it, you know."

"Whatever do you mean?"

"I was born in a workhouse. My mother was a servant. She wasn't married. So you see I can't marry Mr Halley. He would never marry me."

Lydia sat down heavily. Her breath came in gasps.

"You're not even a cousin, then!"

"I am, yes. Through my father Frederick Loft. He seduced my mother."

"He should have the care of you then! Where is he?"

"In the colonies. I don't know where."

"Your telling me about your mother and the workhouse explains a great deal about you. I suspected a low, devious character."

Emily began to feel upset; she had spoken to provoke her cousin, something she should not do. The atmosphere was poisonous. Her cousin was insufferable, but she was going away perhaps for good, and would there be bad blood between them forever? She was somewhat short of relatives. It made her sad.

That night she prayed for a better relationship with Cousin Lydia and she resolved to forgive her.

LADY GOES TO WHITECHAPEL

On Friday afternoon the carriage set off for Whitechapel, with Troy sitting in his place on the box with the coachman. Emily looked out of the front window as it left with some regret. She would have loved to have gone as well, and been introduced to Troy's parents, but Lydia had not extended an invitation, and perhaps it was just as well, as she and Troy probably could not sit together at one table without giving each other loving looks.

The little terraced four-room house in Whitechapel had been scrubbed and polished because the lady was coming to visit. The best tablecloth was laid on the table, the china, a wedding gift thirty years ago from Mrs Troy's mistress, was brought out. She had set out a High Tea of ham and cheese and even had been able to procure tomatoes. A pot of tea, fresh rolls and pats of butter made up the rest of the menu, followed by Christmas cake from the sealed tin.

The visitor received a very warm welcome and was ushered to the best chair. She was her charming self and admired the ormolu clock and numerous other objects acquired by the couple during a lifetime of service.

"Your son is a credit to you both," gushed the wealthy widow, for so they saw her. "I would be lost without him. I wished to pay you a call because he is leaving England with me, as you know, as my personal assistant and aide. A lone woman abroad is at certain risk."

"Jimmy's a good boy and I'm sure he'll 'ave no trouble pickin' up Swiss," said Mrs Troy proudly.

"I beg your pardon? Oh, what a joke! I think it's French they speak in Geneva, though, not – er – Swiss."

They chatted on, with Troy hardly saying a word. His parents were laying the flattery on thick. He was wondering when he should tell them about Emily. He could not do so today at any rate.

"We must take our leave," Mrs Darcy said, regretfully after an hour. "I have not known such warm hospitality in a long time, I hope we can repeat it after we return. I should love to have you visit me."

Troy helped her into her fur trimmed coat and she gave him an affectionate look.

"You see how he looks after me," she said, looking at them with meaning.

Mr Troy handed Mrs Darcy into the carriage and just before he hopped onto the box, Troy turned to his parents.

"I 'ave something to tell you, I'll write tonight, it's easier in a letter – no time now."

"Will we see you before you leave?" Mrs Troy said wistfully.

"Yes," said Troy.

After the carriage left the small court (with a crowd of children running after it and whooping) Mr and Mrs Troy went back into the house, and shut the door firmly. They did not want any nosy neighbours barging in just now.

"What do you think of this?" Mrs Troy asked her husband.

"I think it's a great opportunity for young Jimmy," said Mr Troy. "He'll go places, with her."

"With her? As what? She's in luv with him, Charlie."

"Are you out of your mind, Nell?"

"I'm not – I know. Did you not see the look she gave 'im just now? Wait till you see – he said he'd write – I bet it's about 'er he'll write. Our son will be a gentleman!"

Two days later a letter arrived and Charlie read it out.

Dear Mother and Father

Thank you for putting on such a spread for Mrs Darcy. She was very happy with the visit and has spoken of you since. The reason I am writing is this. It might come as a bit of a shock to you. I am engaged to be married.

"There! I knew it!" Nell jumped up from the chair, spilling her knitting on the floor. "Our lad couldn't be as handsome as that for nothing!"

"My goodness woman, you are amazing." Charlie settled in his chair and rearranged his spectacles on his nose. He frowned as he read on.

My intended is Miss Emily Lucas, from Bristol. She is living here in this house, and that brings me to another matter. When Mrs Darcy goes abroad, the house is to be shut up, and if Emily could stay with you, it would be the best thing. We will be married after I return, in about six weeks. You are the best people to look after my fiancée while I'm gone, Your devoted son, James.

"Miss Emily Lucas from Bristol! I never knew anybody from Bristol," exclaimed Mrs Troy, annoyed and disappointed. "To think I thought it was Mrs Darcy he luved!"

"You said you thought that she luved 'im," Charlie said, folding the letter and putting it back in the envelope. "We'll 'ave to welcome Miss Lucas, whoever she is, she's going to be family, if Jimmy's mind is made up."

"Of course we'll welcome 'er, Charlie. I suppose it's the best thing. If he did marry Mrs Darcy, how would we keep up with the style an' all expected of us? But I was looking forward to telling the neighbours, I was. But I wonder what Emily Lucas is like. I 'ope we get along, 'er and me. Why didn't he say more about 'er?"

HALLEY'S SECRET

Their meetings were becoming emotional, with news breaking nearly every day.

"Mrs Darcy said today we might be three months away," Troy said with resignation. "It'll be more money for us, look at it that way. I 'eard from Ma and Pa. They'll be delighted to look after you while I'm gone."

His parents had not used the word 'delighted' when they had written back to him, but they had said that this was quite a shock but they'd be very happy to look after their future daughter-in-law. Troy read delight into it.

"But three months, Troy! That's too long! Oh if you could just back out now! If I could get my money back from her, you wouldn't have to work at all perhaps!"

"No, I'm the provider," Troy said. His male pride was rattled.

They had slipped out to meet in a small, secluded park about a mile from Cavendish Square. They sat on a bench, wrapped in each others arms. It was a cold day.

"Do you still think she wants me?" Troy asked her.

"I'm sure of it." Emily hung her head in dejection. "She could compromise you in some way."

"What do you mean?"

"I don't know. I've heard of it done, claim that you did something, and make you marry her. You're both free to marry."

"I will be true to you, Emily." He kissed her.

"Troy – could we marry before you go?"

"That's a splendid idea," Troy said suddenly, his arms wrapped tightly around her, his face close to hers. How he longed for her!

Emily smiled happily.

They had three days more. Once the idea had taken hold, it gained momentum, and they jumped up to visit the nearest church, and obtain a marriage license.

"Have you decided where you are to go?" Mrs Darcy asked Emily. Perhaps she was getting a crisis of conscience.

"Yes, I have."

"Where is that, pray? Am I allowed to know?"

"Yes, of course. I am to stay with the Troy's of Whitechapel."

There was a cold silence.

"How do you know the Troy's of Whitechapel?"

"As you do, through Troy."

She longed to tell her the truth! But what if she dismissed Troy? It was the last thing he wanted. Troy still did not believe that Mrs Darcy had any interest in him beyond a trusted servant. She could not risk telling her the truth, but she felt dreadful about deceiving her. She was under her care.

Lydia pondered this disturbing development.

"Are you engaged to James Troy?" she asked bluntly.

"Yes, I am."

There, she had upset everybody's plans now. Troy would be sent for and dismissed. She warned him by leaving a note in the cutlery drawer.

Mrs Darcy called for Troy, but it was for him to bring around the carriage. "I shall not need your assistance with this errand," she told him. Then, frightened that Troy and Emily would use her absence for a tryst, she took Emily with her. She had to pay another call to Mr Halley, but would leave her waiting in the carriage and not disclose her purpose. Emily did not know whose house her cousin was visiting, it looked like a very neglected place, and was very surprised she had a friend there. The coachman had no answers for her.

The meeting between Mr Halley and Mrs Darcy was not as cordial as the last one, as she learned that Mr Halley did not wish to marry anybody.

"I am not the marrying type," he said to her.

"I am aware of that," she said primly. "I am also aware of an incident in Bangalore, many years ago, when you went to the house of a certain Nabob, and something occurred there. My late husband told me of it. You behaved disgracefully – with a boy. There was no end of trouble to cover it up."

He arose suddenly, his face flaming red.

"How dare you! Such a thing never happened! I must ask you to leave!"

"There were rumours around the clubs, but they died down. What if they should resurface? The scandal will ruin you. Oh come now, Mr Halley. What's a little marriage? She can reign in your castle in the North and you can spend all your time here. And – it would of course put to sleep any rumours that might begin circulating about you in this City."

She left a little while later, satisfied, a plan was in place. Emily was freezing in the carriage and was happy to get home. Her cousin was tight-lipped about her errand.

NEW RELATIONS

"I will leave now," Emily announced to Cousin Lydia.

"And how will you get to Whitechapel? Your friend Troy is busy. He cannot take you."

"I shall make my own way, never fear."

"What are you waiting for, then? Go!"

"You have money that should come to me."

There was no reply. Emily left.

Troy had contrived to get his morning's work done in haste, and was at the church.

The marriage license had been obtained and Emily Lucas and James Troy became man and wife in the sacristy of St. James' Church, with the sacristan and his wife as witnesses. Her suitcase was by her side.

He had other errands, and promised to visit her in the evening and spend the night there with her, unknown to Mrs Darcy of course.

"I will be waiting for you," she said simply. "Do not fail to come!"

"Would I miss my own wedding night?" he smiled. "What do you think, Mrs Troy?"

They parted, and she went to Whitechapel, and though she was filled with elation at being Troy's wife, her old fears of strange people and places threatened to overcome it. The streets held hidden dangers; the unknown. How she hated the unknown!

An hour later she was knocking timidly at the door of his house. A middle-aged woman answered it.

"You must be Miss Lucas!"

Emily lost her tongue for a moment, so confused and bashful was she. Troy had not had the time to write them a letter to inform them.

"Actually, we're married now," she said almost apologetically, following her in.

"Married!"

"Yes, she said with some awkwardness, "We just got married – not an hour and a half ago."

A man had gotten up from his seat by the fire, and extended his hand to her. She was bidden to be seated on a chair in front of the fire.

There was a very awkward silence. This is a shock to them, Emily thought. She too felt mute. The clock ticked.

When they did find their tongues she was peppered with questions, and managed to answer, and reassure them that Troy would be along later.

"You call 'im Troy. His name's Jimmy. His father's Troy."

"I'll try to remember," she said.

"And you're from Bristol. Are your parents still there?"

"No, I have a grandfather from somewhere around there – I'm not sure exactly where. He has probably died."

Emily was cagey. How much should she tell them about her origins? Could she really tell them that her mother had not been married and that she had spent the first ten years of her life in a workhouse? But both situations were deeply shameful and she could not bring herself to tell them. They could despise her!

"My mother died when I was young. My father – he is – abroad."

"Where is he?"

"I don't know. I have no contact with him."

This sounded very curious indeed. Mr and Mrs Troy were a couple who had lived all their lives in a very structured society with rules. They were not gentry, but they were respectable and proud of it. There was not a hint of scandal in the family, in hers or his. There was something suspicious about somebody who either would not or could not relate details about parents and brothers and sisters and uncles and aunts. There was a mystery here and they were uneasy. Perhaps when their son came later, they could have a private word with him. But Emily could guess their thoughts and felt ashamed. *I could have told them my father was dead but I did not want to lie.*

"Were you raised with relatives then?"

"I was raised by a great-aunt, my father's aunt."

There was no necessity to mention Yellowhill Workhouse.

The table was set, and she partook of dinner, eel and mashed potato. It did not taste nice and she forced herself to eat the eel, which she did not like.

"Are – were you in service in the Darcy house?" this was the next question. Of course Troy had not mentioned her to them until they had become engaged.

"No, I was not in service – I was visiting Mrs Darcy – she's a cousin."

"Oh, so Mrs Darcy is your cousin!" This was good news to them, and they relaxed. "Why isn't she taking you with 'er to Switzerland then?"

"I don't know – she wishes to go alone."

"Does she know you're married to our son?" Mrs Troy put it bluntly. A picture was beginning to form in her mind.

"No, she does not."

"That's a pity, because if she know you was married, you would go with your 'usband," Mrs Troy pointed out. "What was the rush in marrying? I hope there's nothing – amiss."

"Mrs Troy," her husband tried to quiet her.

"Oh, there's nothing amiss," Emily cried, blushing deeply at the implication, and remembering that she was coming under suspicion because she had not been able to say that her parents had been married. It was cruel! Who were these strangers, related to the man she loved who was now her husband? When she married him, she became one of them and she felt very awkward at being thrust forward into the bosom of a family she did not know. She felt a pressure on her forehead.

"You'll want to see your accommodations," her father-in-law said as he signalled to his wife to show her. She led the way up a rickety, squeaking stairs at the top of which were two doors.

"One for Pa and me, and the other is for you." She threw the door open. It was a pleasant room but smelled of camphor to keep the moths away. The bed, covered in a grey counterpane, was iron framed and sagged a bit in the middle. The counterpane was clean but stained. There was no rug, she would step out onto bare floorboards. A small chest of drawers completed the furniture. The window curtains were a pale orange with white flowers and thin, the same material as the bed curtains, and the washstand with its jug and bowl was old and chipped.

"I 'ope it's orright," Troy's mother said. "You're used to a great deal better."

"Oh, it's fine, thank you very much," Emily protested. In fact she had been thinking that it was very poky and poor. And strange.

"I'll leave you to unpack, then. You can 'ang your gowns in our wardrobe, next door. I left two 'angers there free for you."

"I'm still not over the shock," her new father-in-law said downstairs to his wife. "Our Jimmy married and no notice of any sort."

"No wedding breakfast or any sort of celebration," Troy's mother lamented as she gathered the dishes. "It's not the way I imagined my son's wedding. What do you think of 'er, Charlie?"

"She's cagey, not the friendly sort."

"What did he ever see in 'er? I still think something is up, but we'll know soon enough if there is. She led him on, that's it. Why else would he 'ave to marry in a great hurry? He's not goin' off to a war."

Emily tip-toed downstairs, half-afraid of disturbing her new in-laws, the strangers Troy. She heard the last part of the conversation and her heart dropped.

They don't like me, and I have to live here! Perhaps for a long time if Troy and I can't afford a few rooms of our own! I'm in their way. Will I be rude if I spend a lot of time upstairs by myself? Hurry up, Troy! I need you!

ABDUCTION

"Can I help you with the cooking? I can cook." Emily asked her mother-in-law a little while later. She was sure she sounded awkward. She did not know what she was supposed to do. She had no sewing, no knitting, no books, nothing except her suitcase with a few gowns in it and personal items.

But her mother-in-law was not keen on working with Emily in the kitchen. She had her own ways of doing things and this young woman had her own ways as well. So she declined, thanking her.

"May I have the workbasket?" she asked her. She could not sit around doing nothing!

"Oh, very well. There are some stockings to be mended." So Emily sat down and darned her father-in-law's stockings. A few shirts had frays and tears here and there, she mended them too.

Did I really get married this week? I don't feel married. What is being married supposed to feel like? Why should I not get up and go and be with Troy in Switzerland? But ten pounds would not see her to Switzerland.

She was saved by a neighbour coming in, and she was introduced as *'Jimmy's wife the new Mrs Troy'*. The neighbour was astounded.

"I never 'eard little Jimmy was getting married! Was this sudden, like?"

"Very sudden – he has to go abroad on business, and wished to marry before he left."

The new Mrs Troy was scrutinised. How horrible it was to be stared at as if she were a museum exhibit or an exotic animal at the Zoological Gardens!

Embarrassing questions followed – when did the wedding take place? Today! Only today! Were they, the parents, at it? They weren't! They didn't know! How odd that was, indeed!

Emily wanted to crawl into a shell and stay there as word got around the court and other neighbours piled in, some coming in without knocking as if they lived there.

"I 'ad to get a butcher's at your new daw'er-in-law!" Unfamiliar with Cockney slang, Emily thought it was a rude way of speaking.

She endured being asked questions about herself, her family, her employment, and though she never volunteered the information again that she never knew her father, they too were left with the impression that the new Mrs Troy was stand-offish, cagey and even a snob. Her clothes were better than anybody's in Whitechapel. She longed to be more friendly, but that old tyrant was there in her heart, acute shyness accompanied by a wish that she could disappear.

She knew Troy would be in soon, when he had served dinner at eight. It was a very long day. She felt very impatient to see him.

The door burst open around nine, and Troy came in. He carried a bunch of red roses.

"For my wife," he said, beaming, kissing her on the cheek as his parents gathered around him to congratulate him. The newlyweds supped together, and then the parents announced that they were going to bed.

It was just the newlyweds then, and they kissed, climbed the stairs hand in hand and gave themselves up to love. They clung to each other and stayed awake and whispering most of the night as Troy had to get up at five. Everybody got up to wish him a happy journey – then he was gone. He took Emily's happiness with him. She was uneasy in this new place, her new relations seemed to think she was used to much better and kept apologising.

Troy had left Emily some money. His mother had heard him do this and when Emily did not offer it to her for her keep, it was another thing to feel aggrieved about.

Emily did not know how to please them. A pall hung over the little house. They went to the ship later that day to wave him off. They saw him on the lower deck. He waved his handkerchief. Above his head on the upper deck, Emily spotted Cousin Lydia, who was staring in her direction and smiling with an expression of self-satisfaction. Then the ship sailed, and it was back to the little house in Whitechapel where Emily tried to pretend she was one of the family. But there was awkwardness there – they were polite and made no effort to like her. As always happened when she felt people's disapproval, Emily shut herself into a secret room in her own heart, and grew very quiet. She offered to help the older woman with housework only to have her offers spurned. She wanted to speak but instead she was mute, she had no idea what to talk about. Any conversation she tried to begin was not pursued. Did she have anything in common with her in-laws?

She missed Troy acutely. How was she to endure three months of this awkwardness? Another trouble was that they attended different churches.

"The service is at nine o'clock in the morning," Mr Troy told her as she prepared to go to bed on Saturday evening.

Then she told them that she was not of their denomination, and that she had found out the times of the services in her own church. It was at ten o'clock.

"She's not even of our church," Mrs Troy had another mark against her. "How could Troy 'ave married her, he had no respect for us. And never told us either!"

The following day she walked to St Anne's church on her own. On her way back, she was about to turn into Fairclough Street from Henrique Street when a carriage drew up beside her.

"Oh, Miss, Miss please!" The coachman hopped off the box. "My mistress is very poorly inside the carriage, I just heard 'er cough something terrible and I wonder could you go in and see what you can do for 'er?"

The window curtains were drawn. The coachman opened the door quickly and Emily stepped in.

Two burly figures, one a man and the other a woman, lunged toward her, grabbed her by her arms and wrestled her down onto one of the seats. One of them put a handkerchief over her mouth. The door slammed shut. The smell from the handkerchief was unpleasant and overpowering and her struggles ceased as the coach heaved forward and began to move.

"Did you see that?" gasped a young girl to her friend. They had just turned the corner in time to see the fancy carriage and the coachman opening the door for the new

Mrs Troy, as she was known, to get into it. The door had slammed shut, and the coachman had hopped up on the box and it had then moved smartly away. They had not seen that Mrs Troy had been surprised to be approached, nor did they hear the words the coachman said.

They ran to the court where the Troy's lived and told their story. Mr Troy ran out to the corner, but the coach had long gone.

"What was the meanin' of that?" Charlie Troy said grimly when he returned. "Why did she just get into a carriage like that?"

"I 'ave my own opinion what's 'appened," his wife said, banging the colander with a spoon to get the last of the cabbage out of it. "She wanted 'im, and 'ad to marry 'im to get what she wanted, and didn't realise 'e was as poor as 'e is, and now that she's 'ad 'im, she doesn't want 'im anymore. Come on, let's 'ave our dinner, and think of her no more."

"Maybe she was already married," Charlie said, holding out his plate for a dollop of dripping cabbage to go with his bacon. "Then she can be brought up for bigamy and our son will be free again. There was somethin' about 'er all right, there was."

They went up to her room and found that she had left everything behind. They found ten pounds in an envelope in a drawer.

"Where is she off to, without money?"

"She don't need mint, because the owner of the fine carriage will keep 'er," Mrs Troy said darkly. "Our poor boy was sadly taken in with 'er. How are we going to tell 'im?"

"Not for a time, Nell. He'd be upset gettin' this news from home. Bad news can wait. When he complains tha' she don't write, maybe we'll tell 'im then. "

COMPROMISED

Emily was sleeping for most of the lengthy carriage journey, and later said that she did remembered it but hazily, with some stops, when she was taken from the carriage by the burly woman to an inn where she was told to use the water closet, and then she was taken to a room to eat and drink with the woman and her male companion. They stayed overnight at an Inn, and she was guarded closely.

"Why am I here? Who are you? You have the wrong person! What's going on, please tell me! Let me go!" All of her pleas went unheeded and she was soon forcibly returned to the carriage, there to be sedated again to resume the journey. Night came on as they travelled, a heavy frost settling on the countryside they passed. She shivered with cold.

It was around two in the morning when the carriage finally stopped and this time she was not taken to an inn, but to a fortress the turretted silhouette of which she could make out against the sky.

"It looks like a prison," she cried.

They manhandled her in the large, arched doorway, into a large, cold hall with a chessboard floor. Sconces and lanterns on the wall made dancing lights and ghostly shadows everywhere. A man with a strange gutteral accent met them. He carried a ring with a bunch of large keys on his belt. "Tha'way!" he cried, and they pushed her toward a stairwell and she climbed it, terrified. At last they reached a landing where they stopped. The man took a key and fiddled with the lock, and the wooden door opened with a loud groan. A woman with a candle rose from the darkness to meet them. Emily could see her face, the paleness of it, the hollow eyes and cheekbones, the hardened expression. They were in a bedroom. A large four-poster bed occupied much of the space. Heavy oak furniture and dark walls greeted her eyes. There was a small fire.

"Leave 'er to me, then," said the woman. "Here, drink this." She put down the candle, took a chalice from a little table and pushed it to her lips. The man forced her head back to drink the horrid fluid. She remembered no more of that night.

Emily was awoken early in the morning by the coldness of her limbs and back and the sounds of loud and raucous crows that seemed to be just outside her bed curtains. She was lying on top of the bedclothes. Apart from her boots and cloak, she was fully clothed. As she tried to piece the events of yesterday together in her mind, she heard another sound among the cawing, and this was much nearer – it was a loud and prolonged gasping snore. She sat up. Was that the old woman, keeping vigil in the room? If she was asleep, would she be able to escape from here?

Emily pulled back the bed curtains and planted her feet on the floor. She looked about her, and saw a figure upon the sofa. It was not a woman, but a man. He was in his nightshirt and striped nightcap, sprawled fast asleep on his back, and one arm was resting on the floor, his hands still curled around an empty whiskey bottle. She recoiled with horror. What was he doing here? Tiptoeing closer, she recognised him.

Mr Halley. Thankfully she was dressed – she could try to get away and out of the house. This must be his place in the North, and she had been abducted all the way from London! Her cousin's doing!

She tiptoed towards the door, carrying her boots, but a loud creak on a floorboard was her undoing. She turned to see if he had awoken, and beheld two staring eyes from under the striped nightcap. He struggled into a sitting position and continued to stare at her.

"The door is locked, I have the key," he said, smiling, pulling it out from somewhere on his person and dangling it in front of her.

"Why am I here?" she exploded with emotion. "I was kidnapped yesterday from London, and brought all the way here! Why? I'm not going to marry you, no matter what my cousin says."

"You have to marry me now," he said. He got up and walked toward her. He tottered a little. He was enveloped in the smell of whiskey.

"You 'ave to marry me now," he slurred his speech and laughed.

"No, I can't marry you –"

"We spent the night together – though your virtue is intact – we have to marry now!"

Emily tried to protest again but he interrupted rudely.

"Miss Lucas, please stop your false protests. Your cousin said you're in love with me, but you are too shy to endure a proposal, and she said to bring you here, and put you in my room, and then it will be all arranged, for we are married now, as good as, are we not? My love!"

"We can't be married now –"

"It's arranged for eleven o'clock today, and in a few days we shall set out for London so that I can show off my bride! How I will laugh when I present Mrs George

Halley, to those who said that George Halley was a confirmed bachelor!"

"I can't ever be Mrs George Halley, for I am Mrs James Troy!" Emily was able to make her point at last.

"What?"

"I am a married woman! I married a few days ago."

"Married!" He took a step backwards, and found a dressing gown on a chair with which he covered himself. "Married! I do not believe it. You are joking me."

"I insist it is no joke, Mr Halley. If I were in love with you, would I not be excited and pleased to be here? But I am not and was never in love with you. I am in love with the man I married on the 11th of this month in St James near Cavendish Square."

"Does your cousin know this?"

"No, she does not. She knew I was engaged though."

He looked very displeased. His face grew red and purple and he took the bottle and threw it against the wall. It smashed into smithereens. Emily drew back with a little scream.

"Let me go, I beg you!"

"No, for I have not decided what to do with you."

. . .

He pulled the bell, and a man came five minutes later, during which Emily had sat on a chair and Mr Halley paced about in his dressing gown. At last a footman appeared and the door was unlocked to allow him in.

"Send a telegram to Winters in London. He is to find out about a marriage that took place in St. James between a spinster Lucas and a bachelor Troy, on Wednesday 11th last.

"That's a very long telegram, sir."

"Send it! And tell the vicar to postpone the wedding until the day after tomorrow."

"You still don't believe me, do you? Look!" she held out her hand to show him the ring on her finger.

"I cannot believe I have been so deceived!" he raged. She was frightened of him since he had smashed the bottle. She did not know that, in order to quash any rumours that Mrs Darcy might have begun about him, he had announced his marriage already in London. Now he would be a laughing stock.

He pulled the bell again, and five minutes later another servant appeared, and he ordered her taken from the room and put in East Turret. He had to repeat his instructions to the servant as the man questioned if he had heard right.

SNOWFALL IN THE NORTH

She was marched a long and winding way up to a tiny room in one of the turrets and pushed in. There was no fireplace there. It had a small narrow iron bed with a thin mattress, no pillow and one blanket, and only barely enough room to turn. The walls were stone blocks missing the occasional block to make an alcove. Was this a prisoner's room? The door slammed and was locked from the outside.

She looked out the window which was little more than a slit in the tower. There were no curtains, no glass, and the cold air was rushing in. She was level with the tops of the trees and the crows. They were flying past her as she looked at them. They took no notice of her but she tried to distract herself looking at them. The sky was ominously white. Was it going to snow? It was cold enough!

Was she to get any breakfast? After an hour the door pushed open and a woman servant, the woman who had been in the coach with her, came in with a tankard of sweet tea that had probably been hot when poured but had cooled considerably on the long walk from the kitchen. A hunk of dry bread accompanied the tea. She did not stay to talk, and Emily wolfed it down. She was very hungry even after eating. When the woman (whose name was Tabitha) came back she seemed to be in a chatty mood.

"So you're married," she commented. And then she laughed.

"So we're glad not to 'ave a mistress. We 'ave our own ways here, he's not 'ere often you know. He prefers London and we prefer it for 'im too," she cackled. "A mistress would change everything."

"Will you help me escape?" Emily asked her with desperation in her eyes. "I'm not going to spend the night here, am I? I'll freeze to death! I saw snowflakes earlier."

The woman looked at her thoughtfully.

"Have you any money?"

"Yes, I have, but not here."

"Then tha's no good for nowt, is it?"

"Please give me something to put over the window," she pleaded. "I'm so cold!"

But she went away without promising anything.

Emily was alone with herself for hours and prayed and thought of her husband and the happy hours they had spent together before he had had to go away. She wept, missing him. And what would his parents think? Would they call the police and report her missing? The snow began to fall thickly and silence descended. The crows stopped cawing, hiding in the branches of the tall trees, trying to keep warm. She paced the cell and tried to generate warmth in her body, but she was growing colder by the minute.

Two servants came in the late afternoon and led her out of the turret. At last, she'd be moved to a room with a fire! Her feet were like lead, she could barely feel them. It reminded her strongly of the workhouse when she was a child. Cold, always cold.

They put her in a cart and drove her to the large gate, where they dumped her on the roadway. They turned around and went back in, closing the gate.

Emily was stricken with fear. She could die here. She could freeze to death. Why were people so cruel? She had shown him up, and his pride could not stand it. He was angry with her cousin, but her cousin was not available to punish, so she was punished instead.

She began to trudge downhill – for she guessed that a hamlet or a village lay there. The snow stopped for a while. She trudged on, her feet now soaking wet. It got dark. At last she saw some lights in the piercing darkness. There was a large building with lights. She looked at the plaque on the gate – a layer of snow had already settled on it, but she used her sleeve to clear it away. She could make out the words – Grimton Workhouse. She rattled the high iron gates, shouting hoarsely to the porter. At that moment, she heard a loud groaning noise above her head, and looked up to see a large dark object in a shower of snow hurl itself toward her. She screamed and put her hands up to protect herself.

In the Castle, Mr Halley began to have second thoughts as his anger calmed. He regretted putting her out in the snow, and the following morning asked his men to look for her. They did not find her, but they made an enquiry at the workhouse.

"There was a young woman last evening," said the porter. "She rattled the gate an' I don't know if it was tha' or whether it would've 'appened anyway, but that branch you see there, over by the side, that branch from that tree there, came down on top of 'er. It took three men to move it off 'er."

"Is she alive?" asked Harold.

"If she is she's only jus' about alive," the porter said. "She must've broke some bones. Brayed she wor by fallen branch full of snow, and knocked out, and she's as frostbitten as if she walked across North Pole. She looked dead to me, as was 'elping, but she breathed once. I 'ave to go now, 'ere's another family lookin' to come in out of the snow. That's the third this mornin'. "

TROY IN SWITZERLAND

Troy looked at himself in the mirror and frowned a little. His suit, provided by his employer, fit well. It was the suit a gentleman would wear. It was for his new status as secretary. But he did not know how to be a secretary; he'd never been very good at writing, and his schoolmaster had told him his spelling was atrocious, but Mrs Darcy seemed to think he was ideal for the position.

He felt out of place with his new role. He was not a footman anymore, and he did not know what his function was. Mrs Darcy said she had to 'settle in' and 'get her bearings' before he was to have any work of a secretarial nature. And –

would he do her the honour of dining with her? It was so awful to dine alone, she could not stand it. She would of course bear the extra cost. Chalamet had been given a holiday to see her family in Normandy.

Troy found himself in an uncomfortable situation. His thoughts were faraway. He was conscious of his manners and did not initiate any chats. The Swiss did not lay their tables as the English did, but he did not make a fuss. He called his employer 'Madam' until she told him not to.

"You're not a servant now," she said. "Call me Mrs Darcy."

"When will you 'ave work for me to do, Mrs Darcy?" he asked her from time to time.

"In time, there will be plenty of work. But for the moment, enjoy this new country and the lake and the people we meet. And – which would you like to learn French? Or perhaps Italian?"

He looked astonished.

"Why? Are you thinkin' of going to Italy as well, Madam – I mean, Mrs Darcy? And – will this extend the trip? Why learn a new language for just a few months?"

"I'm thinking of your future, Troy."

"Thank you, Mrs Darcy."

It was very mysterious.

She had to go carefully. Was he still wearing the locket? She did not know. If so, he was skilled at keeping it hidden under his high collar.

. . .

She did all the talking at meals, partly because he did not care to talk. He was a good listener though, and that increased her love for him. It would be very abnormal not to mention Miss Lucas at all, but she did not know what to say without giving away her intense dislike.

But Troy brought up the subject.

"How long does it take for letters to go between here and England?"

"Oh, of course, you are expecting to hear from your fiancée!"

"I wrote to her, I'm just wonderin' when she might get it."

Lydia was secretly annoyed that he had written home without her knowledge. Had he gone to the post office? But no, the concierge had taken it. She was older than he; he was a servant, he had never been outside England, and he was finding his way around quite well. She was not sure why this annoyed her, but it did. However, he would soon find out that his fiancée had married someone else. She would then be his sole consolation, and he would come to depend upon her.

Troy did not like to linger at table, he gave signs of restlessness after eating, and she guessed he was not used to prolonged, leisurely meals. He looked about and shifted in his chair, eager to be gone. If Mrs Darcy had thought about this at all she might have realised that Troy was showing no sign of being in love with her or liking to be in her company for long. But such thoughts were never born in her. She was about to do a great thing for him, raise him up in society, marry him! They might even have a child!

But when this thought occurred to her she thought of Daphne, always with guilt. Again, she lied to herself. Daphne would be unhappy living with her. She was far happier with other children and Mrs Alcott was a motherly woman.

She tolerated Troy's affinity with the hotel staff, most of whom spoke some English. He often stopped to chat with the porter, and even went into the kitchen. He asked the chef if he could do 'pie'n'mash' and then gave him a description of what it was, and the chef was intrigued by this English dish. He went fishing with the manager, which was a little better than going about with the hotel servants, she supposed, though he too was hired help.

After two weeks letters from England began to arrive. There was none for Troy, which disappointed him. She handed the letters over to him to read – Mr and Mrs Sallins reporting that the house was safe and that they were lighting fires to keep the damp away; her Bank reminded her of her debt.

. . .

One morning, before they took breakfast in the dining room, Troy went to Reception to ask if there was any post. He was given two for Mrs Darcy, and glanced at each as he received them. One envelope he thought was in a childish hand; the other in a strong forceful male hand. She received them both with interest, but the one in the childish hand was set aside for now.

Mrs Darcy was sure that the letter she held was from Mr Halley containing the news that he had married Emily, and before she read it, she wondered where and how to break it to Troy. Would she ask him to walk in the gardens? Would she tell him at the lake? She dreaded seeing any shock, distress or grief on his countenance, for that would show her that he had loved Emily. She had convinced herself that Emily had contrived to win his heart by some trick of her own and that now he was away from her, her influence would be much less.

He should be very glad to be rid of her, she thought, opening the letter to receive what she was sure was the best news possible.

Mrs Darcy,

I write in the greatest anger. You have deceived and made a fool of me. Miss Lucas is Miss Lucas no longer; she is Mrs James Troy – yes – that footman you told me of, who all London is talking of, linking his name with yours. You have embarrassed me greatly. I did as you suggested, and she spent the night in my home, and we met in the morning, and she informed me she was married. She has left my Castle and I'm in receipt of the information that she is in the workhouse. Now she is yours, or Mr Troys to rescue. Yours, etc, George Halley.

"Are you all right, Mrs Darcy? You look like you've 'ad a shock. Is it bad news?" Troy had been speaking to her and she had not heard him. The other guests were looking at her in concern, whispering that somebody must have died, or lost at sea, or something dreadful must have occurred, for the English lady was white as the tablecloth and trembling.

Troy made as if to snatch the letter but recovering a little, she folded it quickly and put it in her reticule.

Troy was married! She wanted to scream at him! Why hadn't he told her? Why did he deceive her? But she could not refer to the knowledge she had just gained; there could be no explanation on her part as to why she got a letter written in a man's hand informing her of Troy's marriage and their own wicked plot.

"I wish to go upstairs," she said. "Hold me, Troy. For I will fall if left to myself. Write to Chalamet and tell her I cannot do without her any longer. She must come to me directly. Her address is in my little white book."

Troy helped her to her feet. She was conscious of his strong arm about her waist as she was led to the stairs. On their way across the lobby, he asked the desk attendant to send a maid upstairs to attend to Mrs Darcy. A maid was immediately summoned, and Troy handed over the charge of her in her little private sitting room. She looked pale and her eyes were faraway.

"If there's anything I can do –" he said.

"Nothing, Troy. You are so kind to be concerned for me. What would I do without you?"

"I will help her to her bed," said the maid whose name was Anne. "And get her all she needs."

I suppose I'm free for the day, Troy thought as he thumbed through the book for Chalamet's address. But what can have been in that letter to make her ill?

LYDIA'S NEXT MOVE

Lydia kept to her room for all that day and the next. Troy began to become concerned for her, and standing by her bedside, begged her to tell him what the matter was.

"It is a private matter, I pray you will not enquire of me further." This was all the satisfaction he received.

Alone, Lydia began to rethink her plans. She knew that she still wanted Troy. She wanted to marry Troy. But Troy was already married! But his wife was a resident in a workhouse. Certainly, she ought to stay there. She was born in a workhouse and should die in a workhouse. That was where she belonged.

The fact that Troy had deceived her made no difference. She put all the blame on her cousin. No doubt the order to keep this information from her had come from Emily. He was completely under her control.

Troy still thought that Emily was with his parents. He expected a letter daily!

She got up to write a letter, and rang the bell for the maid, giving her a generous tip to go to the post office with it, for it was very near.

"It is a great secret, do not tell anybody, "She enjoined her. "Not even my secretary."

"No, Madame. Thank you, Madame."

She rose the next day, and asking Troy for his arm, they went for a walk by the lakeside. He was quiet. She did not know why, and refused to give birth to the thought that he was wondering why he had not heard from his wife. Troy was quiet because she had given him a shock and showed him how vulnerable she was. Perhaps he was quiet because he was having some feelings for her.

In London, the Troy's were arguing. Mr Troy felt that he should write and tell his son that his wife had disappeared, voluntarily it seemed. Mrs Troy held out that Troy would come home directly to look for her, thus spoiling his chances with his employer for further promotion or even marriage in the future, for she convinced herself that the marriage to Miss Lucas could be held invalid. Was she of full age? Was not the consent of parent or guardian required?

"He will wonder why he has not heard from us," Mr Troy said, turning over one of his letters to Emily in his hand.

"I'm sorely tempted to open this. There may be one for us in the envelope also."

They opened the envelope and sure enough there was a letter for them, with a short description of their surroundings and hoping to hear from them soon.

Mr Troy sat at the kitchen table that evening and put pen to paper.

Dear Jimmy, it was good to hear from you, we are well here, and the hotel sounds very good and I doubt if your mother and I will ever see the lake you spoke of, it sounds like a fine water no doubt there is as good in England if you go up to Cumbria. Your mother is well. I'm sorry son we had to open the letter addressed to Emily because she is not here. She went away she was seen getting into a carriage on Henriques on her first Sunday here and we have heard nothing from her. Maybe you have heard please tell us if you have and if we did anything wrong to her. God bless you son Your Father and Mother who sends her love as I write. She said your not to forget your prayers.

He posted the letter the following day. Unfortunately, Mr Troy had written Hotel Albert instead of Albertine on the envelope, and when it reached Geneva, it went to the wrong hotel.

GRIMTON WORKHOUSE

The snow brought many indigent families and homeless people to Grimton Workhouse, and it was filled to capacity. The slim resources were stretched very thin.

Emily lay on a pallet on the floor with a dislocated shoulder. A large bandage was wound around her head. She was not conscious. The Matron feared she would lose her toes, for they were a persistent whitish blue colour. Her fingers were swollen and blue and they had had to cut her wedding ring off. The doctor could not get to the workhouse until the weather improved, and she felt the weight of responsibility.

"She's not from these parts, or someone would know 'er," said a stout female ward attendant. "So where's 'er 'usband? She's not in rags, neither, though her skirts are all crinkled, like she slept in 'em. Who is she? Her man's a good-lookin' bloke, in't he?" For the locket around her neck had his miniature, and the attendants gathered around and admired him.

Though unconscious, there were prolonged, low groans from the pallet about an hour after she came in.

"She's getting her circulation back," said another attendant, a contrast to the first, for she was very spare in figure. "Right painful it is too. I 'ad frostbite as a child when I got lost on th'moors, I was out all night, and when they found me I was unconscious, an' I'll never forget th'pain of th' blood comin' back into me feet, never. I roared for hours."

'What are you two chatting here for?" snapped the Matron who had stepped quietly between beds and pallets to get to them unbeknownst. "There's patients to be fed in the long ward! Get on with it!" The women disappeared and Mrs Gilbert looked at the injured woman on the floor and shook her head. "If she dies, an' we 'ave no name for 'er, it'll be a pity. Somebody will come lookin' for 'er sometime, and we won't know. If she dies, we'd best keep the locket, at least for a while."

"Matron, there's a bonesetter in the Men's Section," said another inmate. "His name is Alf Connor."

"A bonesetter, I think we have to do better than that, it's modern medicine we need, not bonesetters," was the retort. But Matron began to think about it. Surely he could do no harm? He was called upon, a pauper because of the drink he imbibed, though he had been sober since admission. He knelt before the unconscious girl, palpated the dropped shoulder, and Matron's heart was in her mouth – and with his thumbs then brought the two together, and the unconscious girl awoke with a loud cry.

"She'll be all right now," he said getting to his feet. "Everything is back where it should be." Matron was not so sure, but she decided that time would tell –

her shoulder looked right again, and she had awoken, which was good, though she fell back into a deep sleep afterwards.

The days passed, the death toll was high at Grimton Workhouse, and the procession to the 'dead houses' at the backs of the wards was steady. But the woman they called 'Mrs Snow' hung onto life. She awoke every day for a few minutes and took some fluid, but when Mrs Gilbert asked her about herself, she looked as if she did not understand. Showing her the locket, with the likeness of the handsome man inside, did not bring any flicker of understanding, only a puzzled frown.

"She's a mystery," Mrs Gilbert said to the doctor. "But she must've come from somewhere! Either the village, or from up the hill. But what's up the hill, only Halley's Castle and the cottages around it? I 'eard of some mysterious goings-on there the night before, a carriage arrived very late at night, and my sister at the Inn heard of it from a servant, and asked the housekeeper about it and was told that no such thing 'appened."

AMNESIA

Days passed and 'Ann Snow' did not appear to make signs of recovery. She was moved to a bed near the attendant's desk. Every four hours or so they turned her and tried to give her a drink of water. She half-woke and groaned in pain. Her fingers and toes had regained their healthy pink colour, so the danger of frostbite was over. The dressing on her head was removed, the doctor was pleased – no sign of infection. They had had to cut her hair to tend the wound and she looked very strange, not that she was aware of it, or cared. Soon she was sitting up and taking spoonfulls of gruel. But she had no idea who she was. She complained of being unable to see, and Mrs Gilbert sent the porter outside the gate in the slush to try to find a pair of glasses, and there was a pair found, but in pieces. They were no good. She would have to do without. She kept her eyes closed most of the time in any case, for her head throbbed and she disliked light.

"No memories at all," said Mrs Gilbert. "She'll have to stay with us. But will she be able to do any work? Will her shoulder be any good – maybe she's injured for life."

While Emily was drifting in and out of consciousness, she became aware that she was in a workhouse. The smell of gruel, of urine, the hard bed, the nearness of the next bed, the footsteps on bare boards – all told her before she opened her eyes.

Where's Mama? This was her constant thought, and wondering why her mama was not coming to her. *Where's Maria? Do I have to get up today and scrub the lodging houses? I don't want to! I don't feel well today!*

She voiced her anxieties one morning and Abbie and Tina looked at one another.

"Who said anyfink about scrubbin' lodgin' houses? You're not going anywheres until you're well," said Abbie the stout attendant.

"Who are you?" asked Tina.

"I'm from here."

"Here? Whereabouts? Nobody knows you."

"Why do you talk nonsense? I was born here, wasn't I? Isn't this Yellowhill?"

"Yellowhill? I don't know any Yellowhill." Mrs Gilbert was on hand without delay. "You came in 'ere on a snowy night, and you were hit by a falling branch at the gate. We don't know where you came from. Did you walk up from th'village of Grimton? Or did you walk down from Halley's Castle?"

"I don't know what you're talking about. I was born in Bristol, and why are you telling me I'm not in Bristol? I was born here in this workhouse. Where's my mother?"

"What age are you, luv?" asked Mrs Gilbert.

"I don't know, ten or eleven." Patients and attendants were listening attentively, a titter rippled around the ward.

"No my dear, you're a grown woman. And you've lost your memory. You're miles from Bristol in the north of England. You're married, you know, because we had to cut the ring off your finger. This is your 'usband."

Emily looked at the portrait of the handsome man in the locket.

"I don't know him at all," she said.

Mrs Gilbert bustled away.

"She's far gone," the attendants muttered to themselves. "She's for the locked ward, she is.

"Shh. Gilbert's comin' back!"

The Matron had a looking-glass and put it into Emily's hands.

"There, look at yourself in that."

Emily beheld a woman's face in the glass. It was a little like her mother's face but not handsome like hers. She took off her mob-cap and saw half of her hair shaved off, an ugly scar on her skull and an unhappy, puzzled frown upon her face. She had dry, cracked skin, crusted eyelashes and pale lips. She thrust the mirror back at the matron and lay back on her pillow, upset. She was a stranger to herself. Where was her husband, and how did she end up in a place in England which was foreign to her?

Mr Halley was on the Board of Guardians for the workhouse but he rarely attended meetings as he spent most of his time in London. Abduction was a serious crime and he was very relieved to hear that the girl had lost her memory. For the 'mystery woman' was news all over Grimton. He was worried about the telegrams though. The postmaster was a discreet man. A sum of money changed hands and he was rewarded for his complete discretion. Halley's Castle staff was threatened and bribed to stay silent also. He felt safe and returned to London as soon as the snow melted.

BAD NEWS

"A letter for you, from England," Mrs Darcy had received the mail first, and she handed the long-awaited envelope to Troy.

"At last!" he exclaimed. It was three long weeks later and he had been getting very anxious.

She watched him carefully as he opened and read it. His face turned a shade of white and he shook all over.

I'm sorry for inflicting this on you, she thought silently, but it will be for the best. *Really it will. You may grieve now, but you and I shall be happy together.*

"Are you well, Troy? What is wrong?" He looked everywhere but at his companions, stuffed the letter into his pocket and got up and went away, wordlessly, out the front door of the Hotel.

"It must be bad news, Madame! Someone is dead!" Chalamet wrung her hands. "He might be going to the lake! Oh, who is dead? Not his mother, or father – no one does not throw oneself into the lake for them – dear as they are –!"

"Stop talking nonsense!" Mrs Darcy interrupted her. She was genuinely alarmed – this scene had not played out as she had planned it – he was supposed to have told them the bad news, not run off like that! Now she was alarmed also, on two fronts – one, that he might do himself harm and two, that *he really loved Emily.* For the letter was telling of her death. She got up hurriedly and called for the concierge.

"Make someone follow him, lest he do himself harm! He has had bad news!" She could not make herself understood, and Chalamet came to her assistance, and told the man in very rapid French, using twice the words necessary, that Monsieur was about to do away with himself because of a death, and he should be followed to make sure he came to no harm.

They remained in the lobby for about an hour until Henri returned with Troy in tow. He had been weeping. Mrs Darcy was again annoyed. She did not want to acknowledge that Emily meant so much to him. It was very maddening. But she could not pretend that she knew anything, of course.

"Troy," she said, getting to her feet, "I understand you have had a dreadful shock. May we know what it is?"

Troy seemed unable to speak, so Henri spoke instead.

"His wife, she is dead."

"His wife!" Chalamet gasped. "But he –"

"Oh dear, I am sorry to hear it," Mrs Darcy said. "Who was the letter from?"

"My father."

"But is he sure?"

"Yes. They had the funeral."

"What happened? May I –"

Troy fumbled for the letter and handed it to her. She read it silently.

Dear James, I write with a heavy heart to you today. Your wife Emily has met with a serious accident and died as a result of her injuries. We held the funeral. Your mother is distressed by it all. We urge you to stay where you are, nothing is to be gained by sailing home from the continent. We have taken care of everything. Fondest regards, and deepest sympathies, your Father.

"I will be leaving for England tomorrow, Mrs Darcy," he said. "You see my father gives no details. I hand in my notice today."

"Troy, your father writes –"

"I must go to England," he insisted quietly.

He asked for the letter back, put it in his pocket and turned and went upstairs to his room.

Mrs Darcy was in a great panic when she went to her chamber. She called her maid.

"I have had such a shock," she told her. "I must retire to bed for the day. Help me into my nightgown, and put out my silk lilac dressing gown."

"Yes, Madam."

"I will lunch here. For I am not at all in the mood to meet people in the dining room. Poor Troy!"

"I never knew Troy was married, Madam! It was a complete surprise to me to hear of a wife! Did you know, Madam? Who is she?"

Mrs Darcy started. She had made a mistake! She had expressed no surprise at all at the mention of a wife. Would Troy notice?

Probably not, she reasoned.

"Yes, of course I knew," she lied, to save face. A servant was supposed to ask permission to marry, or at least to have the courtesy to tell his employers.

Chalamet became quiet. Her usual chatter was gone. As she prepared the lotions to remove her mistress' cosmetics, Mrs Darcy interrupted her.

"I shall leave it on for now," she said. "If I feel better later I may get dressed again and go for a walk."

She dismissed Chalamet and brushed her own hair, touched up her makeup around the eyes, frowned at a wrinkle, and splashed herself with eau-de-cologne.

She had not meant to go this particular route, but needs must. She ordered madeira with two glasses and asked the porter who brought it to fetch Mr Troy to her. He raised an eyebrow but she placed silver in his palm.

EYES OPENED

"**Y**ou have need of me, Madam?" Troy stood before her, his suit crumpled, his hair in disarray, his face red, his collar hastily done up. He looked at her and yet seemed not to see her.

She came toward him, her silk dressing gown floating about her. He looked at it dumbly, and took a step backwards.

"I only wish to offer you my deepest sympathies," she said to him. "I have been taken ill at the distressing news. You say you must leave immediately for England. Have you enquired about the trains?"

"There's one leaving at eight o'clock tonight," he said numbly.

"Please allow me to be of service to you in the meantime," she said soothingly. "Please do me the honour of seating yourself in that chair, and tell me all about your dear wife."

He sat down, but a long pause ensued.

"You knew, then?" he said.

"Yes, she confessed to me, unable to keep a secret like that from me, Miss Lucas wrote and told me."

He looked sharply at her.

I've made another mistake. Why would she write to me and not to Troy? I have to get this done today, for if I do not, I will have lost him forever.

"You must excuse my appearance," she said rather coyly. "But Chalamet thought I looked dreadful and persuaded me to rest, and then I sent her away. Then I began to think of you and of your great burden, and certain things occurred to me that you should know, at least before you board the train for the ship back to England."

He looked at her expectantly, but it was a sort of look that seemed he was suffering her rather than welcoming her concern.

She poured two glasses of Madeira and held one out to him. He hesitated before accepting.

"It is good for shock," she said. "Now this is what I wanted to say to you, Troy. It is of course the most understandable thing that you should wish to drop everything and return to England just now. But your father advises against it, and I feel you should think on that. Your father wants the best for you. He knows you have opportunity in my employ, and wishes to remind you of it."

Troy was silent, he sipped his wine, twirling the stem about absent-mindedly. Sometimes she wondered if he was listening. His eyes were casting about the room as if he were not.

He is not in love with me, she thought despairingly. *But I cannot part with him! I cannot! His wife is in a workhouse in Durham – well out of the way. Why should I not take advantage of the opportunity? He is here with me! He shall stay!*

It was almost lunchtime and she pulled the bell and without asking him, ordered it to be brought up for two. There was more wine with the lunch of grilled salmon and roast potatoes. Troy ate at her urging, and she poured him another glass – of brandy this time.

"Will you think on it, Troy?" she urged him. "I need you. You have a future with me. A very real future, with status, independence and –dare I say it –

something more?"

He looked at her directly now, his light brown eyes keenly fixed on her. What thoughts were behind those fine eyes? Did he despise – or see a future with her?

"I cannot bear to lose you, Troy. And if you go, I shall lose you. I know I will."

He looked at her again, puzzled. Had his friends been right about her? Had dear Emily been right? Did this woman have romantic designs upon him? He was not so much attracted as repulsed. Her face he could see was heavily made up, an older face caked with powder.

"I'm not so much older than you, you know," she continued. "I'm twenty-five. There are a few years, yes. But please consider staying, for I shall be lost without you, Troy."

Troy knew this was a lie, for Emily had told him her true age.

"If you 'ave no further need of me, I shall go." He put down his glass and stood up, and her heart sank to her silk slippers.

"Troy, do not go, I beg you." She came closer to him. She wound her arms around his neck.

"Mrs Darcy," he said, pushing her gently away. "You 'ave 'ad too much wine."

"You will not go. I am responsible for you," she said. "This morning, you might have harmed yourself."

"I 'ad no intention of that."

"But I will never forgive myself if you are overcome. Please stay here where I can watch you. Please sit down again and forgive my excess of emotion just now. Troy – do you think the loss of poor Emily is not my loss too? I had grown very fond of my dear cousin. Let us talk of her. Tell me how you two managed to form a courtship under my very eyes! You must have been very clever, for I never suspected a thing! Wherever did you meet?"

He began to talk of Emily, his dearest Emily, and the afternoon wore on. She hated every word he said, every laugh that escaped him at a fond memory, every tear that came to his eye. Her blood boiled when she heard of their secret meetings in the house after everybody had gone to sleep, but she remained calm and sweet. And he stayed. Then he began to be quiet and reflective. His eyes closed. He was sleeping. She took the glass from his hand, and sat on the arm of his chair, taking his head on her bosom. She stroked his burnished hair – she felt dreamlike. A sudden knock came to the door, she started up to her feet. It was Chalamet who without waiting for an answer, was letting herself in.

"You are not required this evening!" she said, whirling about to see if the knock had awoken Troy. It had not. Chalamet stared before she curtseyed and shut the door again.

Troy was deeply asleep, exhausted. It was eight o'clock. If he were to stay the night, there would be a compromising situation and he would have no way out of his obligations.

She went to her bed and blew out the candle and slept.

CHALAMET'S REGRET

Troy stirred uneasily, his head was at an awkward angle, and it was now giving him pain. He rubbed the back of his neck.

Something had woken him up – an uneasy dream. He had been hearing words in his dream. *Something's not right. Something's not right with the letter.*

He fumbled for the letter he had received that morning, and seeing a candle and matches, he obtained enough light to read by. There was a figure on the bed in the room – Mrs Darcy. She appeared to be sleeping.

Somethings not right. He opened the letter, smoothed it out and holding the candle close, re-read it. The problem leaped out at him. His father never wrote a formal letter, he wrote as he spoke, so that you could almost hear his voice. This letter had nothing of his father's voice. His father wrote long sentences, one running on another. This was not written by his father. There were no details of the accident or the nature of it. And the salutation of James – never. It was Jimmy. Always Jimmy. The paper was wrong too. It was thicker and smoother than the writing paper available in Whitechapel. It was expensive!

What was the meaning of this? A letter purporting to be from his father with the devastating news that Emily was dead! This threw the devastating news into grave doubt. Emily was probably alive – she was almost certainly alive! But in some kind of trouble, so that she could not write to him. And somebody meant him to think her dead and to stay away from England.

He gazed at the figure on the bed, as if the answer lay there. He was sure it did. Then the reality of his own presence in the room hit him – if he were here overnight, it would be a disgrace or – they would have to marry. Perhaps the Hotel staff would not even tolerate this kind of situation. He got up, blew out the candle and let himself out. He went to the lobby where he would be sure to be seen, had a little chit-chat with Henri who asked him if he was all right, ordered a drink from the bar and went to his room.

The boat train had left, but it was just as well he was not on it. He needed to find out more before he quit Switzerland. He hardly slept that night, a combination of hope and determination and impatience kept him awake. Early in the morning, he knocked at Chalamet's door in the women servants' wing.

"Troy!" she came to the door and tightened her shawl about her over her nightgown. "Are you all right?"

"I need your help today," he said. "Can you come early to the servants' dinin' hall? I 'ave a favour to ask you."

"Of course," she replied.

The servants had a hasty cup of coffee in the early morning before going to their work. Chalamet was drinking hers when Troy appeared.

"Chalamet, you didn't know my late wife was Miss Emily, did you?"

"No! Our Miss Emily? Miss Lucas?"

"She was my wife. We married the day before I left England."

"Oh Troy, I am so sorry! And Madam knew and never said a word! Oh, Troy. I am so sorry about Miss Emily – Mrs Troy, I mean. And I am very ashamed of myself – the way I used to speak of her when she came first to London..." tears filled her eyes. "I offended deeply against charity and I confessed it to God long ago – but now I feel such regret, you must think so poorly of me."

"Don't think of it," Troy said kindly, as he dragged out a chair and sat in it. A kitchen maid came and poured him a cup of coffee.

"You were right to get up and leave the table at the kind of talk I was making – Miss Emily was so kind to me after my mother died, then I felt very sorry indeed –" she went on.

"You two became very good friends, Chalamet."

"Yes, we did. What did you wish to ask of me? I will do anything for Miss Emily's husband."

"The favour I want, Chalamet, is for you to take Mrs Darcy from the Hotel this afternoon, and keep her away for about an hour."

She looked at him with surprised eyes.

"Why? Why do you want me to do that?"

He shifted uncomfortably in his chair. He was not sure how much he could trust the lady's maid. He said nothing.

"I saw you yesterday in her chamber, sleeping in the chair." Chalamet began. "I did not like to see that." Troy looked at her with questioning eyes.

"Be careful, unless you want..." her voice trailed off. "I am leaving her, I wish to go and look after my father, and I do not plan to go on with her, for her behaviour is very bad – how she –"

Troy did not say anything, but held her gaze.

"You are a married man, and she knew it, and yet she talked of taking you to Italy and she told me that you would never wish to go back to England, but stay with her! Yesterday I find out she knew you were married!

Now you are free, but she does not deserve you. She is very selfish, is my lady."

"Chalamet, Emily is not dead. That letter was not written by my father, or my mother, or anybody I know. Somebody wished me to believe 'er dead, so that I wouldn't go back to England and – perhaps so I would think myself free to marry."

Chalamet was silent.

"I will make her go out this afternoon with me. I will make something up."

"Another thing – I will need to examine her personal papers. Does she lock them up?"

"Yes, everything of value is in the drawer beside her bed. It is locked. I will obtain the key for you. It is the least I can do."

"I'll watch for you going out. And if she asks for me today, tell her you don't know what my plans were. I don't want to see 'er."

TROY INVESTIGATES

T roy waited until he saw the two women walk out of the Hotel Albertine, and then he went to Reception.

"I would like the key to Mrs Darcy's room," he said. "She wishes me to obtain some papers for her."

Henri handed it to him.

In the room, Troy unlocked the drawer by the bed, and there was the letter he had handed to her a few weeks ago, the letter in the forceful male hand. He sat on the bed and read it, his face becoming contorted with anger. Mr Halley abducted his wife, took her to his home, and turned her out when he found out she was married. And it was upon Mrs Darcy's instructions that he did this.

At least he knew where Emily was! That was a great relief. But why had not his parents written to him of her disappearance? Perhaps they had, and the letter had been intercepted or gone astray. That must be it. Under the letter was the other letter written in the childish hand. Curious, he opened it.

Dear Mama, why do you not write to me? I was eleven years old on the 2nd of January and I thought there would be a letter. I try to be good. I have not seen you for one year. I had no letter from you for ages. I am sad. Mama, please write. Your loving daughter, Daphne.

The sadness of the child who wrote this letter pierced him, for it told him the character of the woman he had worked for, liked and trusted. If she could treat her own child, her daughter, like that, it was very likely she treated others worse.

Hidden underneath a silk muffler he found a large envelope, the wax seal broken. It had a direction on it - *To Cousin Lydia for Emily's expenses*, and a letter from 'Cousin Althea'. He counted seven hundred pounds. Emily's money – the sum that was supposed to have been spent on her and instead was kept by Mrs Darcy for her own use. He took fifty pounds out of the envelope and laid it in the drawer. With that and her jewellery, she would face no hardship. He placed the envelope and the rest of the money in his pocket.

He took the letter pertaining to Emily. He unchained his pocket watch, a gift from her, and laid it beside them. He went to his room and retrieved every gift she had given him – a fountain pen, cufflinks, and a snuff box, and then he changed into a worsted jacket and trousers of his own that he had brought with him. They were too shabby for the Hotel. He put them on and brought the two good suits and shirts provided by her to her room and dropped them on the floor. He had already taken note of Mr Halley's London address.

He wondered what to do with the little key Chalamet had given him – she would most likely be in trouble. It could not be helped. He left it on the dressing table.

He left the room key in the suite and closed the door. He left by the back entrance and ran to the railway station, catching the first train going to France, for he could be branded a thief as soon as Mrs Darcy saw the loss of her money. Hopefully he could be in Calais before the police caught up with him. Though he had only taken what was his wife's, the police might not see it that way and he did not relish the thought of spending time in a Swiss jail.

When Mrs Darcy returned and Chalamet asked for the room key, they were told that Mr Troy had it.

"You may leave me, Chalamet," Mrs Darcy said to her, smiling to herself.

"Yes, Madam." Chalamet made her way to her own quarters and Mrs Darcy ascended the stairs to her room confident of finding Troy there waiting for her with love in his eyes and needing her comforting arms. How silly of her to have left him last night! When she had awoken, he had gone.

She opened her door but did not see Troy. She saw the suits upon the floor and the glittering objects upon the bed.

She picked up a note:

I know all and I have taken back what is Emily's. Do not try to contact me ever again.

He was gone and so was her money. Her world changed in that moment. She screamed and threw a hysterical fit so that Chalamet had to be called by the staff. A doctor was summoned. She was inconsolable. He gave her a heavy sedative. She tossed and turned for three days, Chalamet, overwhelmed and fearing she would not be paid, took two weeks wages and disappeared.

Three days later the Hotel staff told Mrs Darcy to leave. She was disrupting the peaceful atmosphere and the other guests had complained. She had to move into a very inferior boarding house which was detestable to her.

STOCKTON-ON-TEES

Emily asked Matron for her locket back, and she was given it, reluctantly.

"Don't let it out of your sight," Matron warned her. "There are people here who would take it, and pass it to the outside, and you'd never see it again."

Emily was grateful for the advice. Every day she gazed at the picture in it, asking: 'Who are you? Who am I?'

Her shoulder healed, and she moved to the laundry where she was to work. She still had no memory of anything. One day she was hanging out the sheets when a murder of crows began to get very noisy high up in a tree. They were loud and argumentative. She felt terrified and did not know why, she began to sweat and wanted of all things to run back inside. Why would she feel dreadful about a flock of harmless birds?

"Why are you affrighted of the birds? You should hear 'em up the hill there, they're noisier than a pack of barkin' dogs. Up in Hally's Castle."

Was I there? Emily asked herself. I wish I could remember!

Growing more restless with the longer days, Emily did not want to stay in the workhouse. She desperately wanted to find out more about herself, and yet, would they allow her to leave? She was not at all sure that they would. She felt trapped here in this place and wanted to go home to Bristol. For Bristol was surely home...

I'm going to make my way there, she thought. Even if I have to walk all the way. It's on the other end and the other side of England, but I will go. I will. It pleased her that she remembered her geography lessons from when she was a child there. They must have educated her well at the workhouse, but that part puzzled her. Did she go to a proper school then?

One February day she saw her chance when the gates were open wide and she was sent on an errand to the admitting office, which was just inside the gate. She had nothing with her but the clothes she stood up in. She walked casually to the gates and went out. Had the porter seen her? His broad back was to the window – he was engaged in something that absorbed him. The birds were singing merrily in the trees as she made her way down the hill towards the village. North, south, east, west – she had to go south to get to her destination. Her only possession was her locket. She was confident that kind farmers' wives would help her on the way.

She had difficulty seeing far ahead and her eyes got tired easily, a result of not having spectacles. By now she was sure she had worn them sometime.

She walked for a few hours. Carriages, carts and a few faster walkers passed her, and a flock of sheep accompanied her for a mile. She did not talk to anybody, she kept her head lowered. But after a few hours, she began to think this journey would not be an easy one. It was too late to turn back now. She had to get food and a place to sleep. She espied a farm and all her fears of strangers and new people threatening to overwhelm her as she approached the farmhouse. Her needs won out and she went to the door. She was directed to the back where the farmer's wife gave her bread and milk and told her she could sleep in the barn. "Poor creature," she said to her husband. "She 'as the workhouse uniform on her. I'll give 'er some clothes and send 'er on 'er way tomorrer. She's gone in the head, maybe. She 'as a locket she showed me and said it was 'er husband in the picture. I doubt it. But I humoured 'er."

The following morning saw her being brought into the warm kitchen and enduring a lecture from the farmer's wife while she ate fresh scones and warm milk.

"You are mad, girl. To walk to Bristol! If you stay a week 'ere, I'll give you the fare as far as Stockton-on-Tees. Can you work?"

"I can scrub very well," she said proudly.

"Well, then, I 'ave plenty for you to do."

A week passed, and she was true to her word. She could scrub and polish to a shine, though her shoulder ached. The farmhouse never looked cleaner. Though the work was hard, Emily found satisfaction in doing something useful. Mrs Botham was as good as her word, she gave her the fare to Stockton-on-Tees and some clothes and a bully beef sandwich. Mr Botham had to go to the nearest town, and there was a railway station there. She took a lift from him on the cart and boarded a train for Stockton-on-Tees. She knew she had travelled on a train before; she wished she could remember it. When she alighted at the railway station, she did not quite know what to do next but she knew she was hungry. She wandered outside the station building and looked about her carrying her little flour sack bundle of spare clothes.

Unfortunately, her hesitancy was noticed by a pair of drunks, who came over to make vulgar suggestions, but she walked away, up a long street, a wide street.

MAID-OF-ALL-WORK

S tockton was a large thriving market town, but she did not feel strange there. It was on a river and she could hear sounds of what she knew to be shipping. I have lived in a town like this before, she thought, perhaps it was Bristol.

It was market day, and the shambles was busy, but she did not like the sights or the sounds of animals being slaughtered, so she took another street, wondering what she was going to do.

You should have thought about this, she reprimanded herself. You have to get a job, or beg.

She did not know where to begin. Added to her trouble was the fact that she could not remember ever applying for a job before, not a proper one at least. She knew she could scrub and that was all.

She knocked on a door and asked the servant who opened it if there were any scrubbing jobs available.

"No, tha's what I'm 'ere for innit, a maid-of-all-work, I am." The door shut –

but she knew now what she want to be. A maid-of-all-work.

She went down a row of what she thought were respectable looking terraced houses, knocking on each door, and receiving a negative response in each. It was getting dark and she was hungry, so in the last house, she asked for some food and received a slice of bread and butter and a cup of water. It was something but she had nowhere to spend the night so she turned her steps toward the centre of town again.

Going up to the marketplace, she found the square a stinking mess of animal offal and blood, rotted fruits and vegetables, and stalls being dismantled. Gradually the stall owners packed up and disappeared. She smelled food cooking. The slice of bread had not satisfied her. But there was nobody about now; she sat in a doorway and weakened from her day and the lack of food, fell asleep.

"Do you want to earn a shilling?" a man woke her up. He was one of the drunks she had met earlier.

"What doing?" she asked.

He laughed but there was an impatience in his laughter.

"A shilling and sixpence, then? It's more than what you'd get from a sailor, they're a mean stingy lot."

"What do I have to do?" she asked, rubbing her eyes.

The drunk seemed to think this was very funny and called some other men over who seemed to appear from doorways and corners, and she became afraid of them. They loomed above her and she shrank into the doorway, wishing it would open so that she could escape to safety.

She touched her locket. It gave her strength to think about her husband, whoever he was.

A window opened above her head and a bucket of foul smelling fluid descended upon the heads of the men gathered about. They shrieked and cursed and quickly dispersed. She had escaped the ugly shower, however. The front door opened and she beheld a man in his nightshirt and cap, carrying a candle and looking very angry.

"So you're the cause of it," he bellowed. "I'll not 'ave your likes 'ere, this is a respectable 'ouse, begone!"

"If you please, sir, I'm desperate. I lost my memory and do you have work for a maid? A maid-of-all-work?"

"You can stay in th'doorway, and clean up tha' mess at daybreak. Swill some water on it and scrub it."

"Oh yes, sir, I will sir! I can scrub!" She waited until dawn crept over the town and when the door jerked open she was given a pail of water and a bristle brush and told to clean up the mess. She did so, and was rewarded with Twopence with which she was able to purchase a fresh roll from the bakery.

The remainder of the day was very long and bleak. *I shall have to go to a workhouse again if I can't get work,* she thought. She went toward the riverside where there were lodging houses and tried them. In the fourth one, she was told of a vacancy in Eccles Yard, in a place called 'Barnes Lodging House for Men.' The yard was more an alley than a yard, and the place she was looking for was a decrepit building of thick stone walls with a large front door with a sign over it.

She was in luck! Mrs Barnes took her on straightaway, for they needed help there and then to get supper for the men expected to come in from the railways at any moment.

"Can you cook and clean, Mrs Snow?"

"Yes," she was not about to say no – in her desperation, she decided that if the woman wanted a cook, she would say she was a cook.

"Will you want lodgin' 'ere too?"

"Yes, I do, please!"

"Do you 'ave any character?"

She did not know what was meant. "I have a good character," she said, which made the woman laugh.

"Orright, well we'll take you on then. A pound a month, with your bed and board and any breakages and damage taken out of it. No perks. If I find you spearing the meat to get fat to sell I'll throw you out. Go upstairs to top of th'house, th'first door on the left, and take water with you to get cleaned up and come back downstairs, and you'll find an apron behind this door."

"I'm hungry, could I –"

"Here, come in th'kitchen, 'ave a bit o'soup - Bedelia, get this girl some soup. She'll 'elp with the cookin' and general duties."

RECOGNITION!

S he discovered with some relief that she would not
have to cook that evening, for supper was a cold
one, consisting of ham and pea pudding and thick
hunks of bread. She espied foodstuffs in the pantry and
the scullery and knew instinctively that she would know
how to prepare them. *I must've cooked some time*, she
thought to herself. *I have been taught to cook.* It felt hopeful
to be able to put pieces of herself back together. *Was I a
cook?*

She worked quietly, ignoring the lodgers and the noise
around her, and her employer seemed pleased. Bedelia,
the other servant, was a young woman who kept saying
she reminded her of someone.

"Bedelia, stop chatterin' and see to th'eggs," her employer
commanded early the next morning. "You see that new

girl Ann Snow there. She's 'ardly uttered a word since she started. She gets down to th'work and tha's that. I wish you could follow 'er example."

"I was only telling Mrs Snow that I thought I know'd 'er, Uncle."

"How could you know 'er!"

"Maybe it was from time I was in London," Bedelia said with a pout. "She reminds me of someone." As soon as her uncle was out of her sight, Bedelia began her investigation again.

"Mrs Snow, was you ever in London?"

"No, I wasn't. I don't think so."

"What do you mean?"

"I don't remember if I was. I had an accident and lost my memory."

"Your voice. Now I know I know you. I met you in London."

Emily got up quickly from her position by the open fire where she had been stirring a large pot of porridge hanging from a hook. "You knew me? Are you sure?"

"Yes, you're as familiar as anything!"

Emily quickly opened the locket around her neck.

"Did you know him too?" she asked eagerly.

Bedelia's jaw dropped and her hand clutched her chest.

"That's Troy, th'footman!" She pointed at him. "It is!"

"Troy! Is that his name, then? Troy?"

"That's 'im, I'd know 'im anywhere. But why 'ave you got 'im around your neck?"

"I'm married to him."

"Married to 'im! You couldn't be!"

Delia began to laugh heartily. She seemed unable to contain herself and put her apron to her eyes, continuing to laugh.

"Oooh tha's too much, tha's too good, it is! I'll die!"

Emily became alarmed, and offended, and maddeningly curious.

"What's so funny, Bedelia?"

"I know who you are, and oh, I 'ope you are married to 'im, cos you wiped 'er eye good and proper! Oh, this is sweet to th' ear indeed, to 'ear she din't get 'im, after all, the witch!"

"Whatever are you talking about? Who are you talking about? Whose eye? Who is she, the one you call a witch?"

Bedelia pointed to her.

"You're Miss Lucas as was! The mistresses cousin. Tha's the witch, Mrs Darcy, who threw me out on th'street, because she knowed – I mean she thought –

that I 'ad a fancy for Troy, an' it was knowed all around she wanted 'im for 'erself. Oh, I wish I'd seen 'er face when you told 'er you was gettin' married to 'im! But 'ow on earth did you end up as you are? And where's Troy?"

"I wish I knew," Emily's heart was beating fast.

"Are you sure you married 'im?"

"After my accident they had to cut a wedding ring off my finger."

Bedelia chuckled again.

"I'll tell you summat, I liked 'im too. But don't worry, I'm over 'im. I'm courtin' a butcher now, Mr Hopkins who supplies our meat. We're gettin' married next year. They called me Delia in London – now do you remember anything?"

"Girls!" Uncle Dickie charged in. "Wha's th'delay? The men are out there goin' mad! They 'as to get to work! Get tha' breakfast out this minute! Do I smell burnin' porridge? Bedelia I'll blame you if eggs are 'ard as bullets! Confound ye, wimmen, when ye start chattin'. All I'm hearin' is laughin' and jokin' as if you were at a Fair. All the same y'are."

The girls flew back to their tasks and Emily had to force herself to concentrate on ladling the hot burned porridge into twelve bowls without scalding herself. Her name was Lucas! Her husband was Troy! Today was a wonderful, hopeful day! She hoped that the burned porridge wouldn't be the cause of her being on the streets again as soon as breakfast was finished, but Bedelia told her aunt, Mrs Barnes, that the talking was all her fault and she please keep Mrs Snow on.

CLUES

"Your Christian name is Emma, no tha's not reet, it's Em'ly. Emily Lucas," Delia said that afternoon when the girls were 'making beds' upstairs. In truth the beds were bunks, very narrow and all they did was straighten the grubby sheets and pull the blankets up, and if they saw a flea, hunted it down.

"You came from somewhere, Bristol you say it must've been, but your cousin, Mrs Lydia Darcy –" Delia paused to deliver a punch to a pillow, causing a shower of dust that made Emily sneeze. "She wor a 'ard one, she wor. You wor livin' with your aunt in Bristol, and I remember she died, an' you were supposed to go shoppin' that day and you din't."

Emily was then flooded with memories of her great aunt Althea. In her mind's eye she saw her old, wrinkled face framed in her nightcap, and she was sitting up in bed in her darkened room. Then she saw another face – her governess, Miss Browne, taking her for walks...there was Sarah, the unflappable maid, and Mrs Anderson the cook, and Mick who did odd jobs. Bristol came back clear as day. Of course she had learned to cook there, and sew and mend and history and geography too...but after that, the missing months of late last year, when she had fallen in love and married – she longed to remember them.

"Get me the feather duster," Delia said, and seeing that Emily looked vaguely around, added: "You used to wear spectacles. That's why I din't recognise you at first, that and you've got a bit fat."

"Fat! Me!"

"Yes you've filled out a bit."

"What else do you remember?"

Delia remembered with some guilt the hilarity in the servant's hall at Miss Lucas' expense – she would not mention that of course.

"Do you remember Madam's French maid? Charlette - no, Chalamet."

She frowned and shook her head.

Delia named other people but she did not remember any of them. Those weeks were still hidden.

"After I was dismissed from Cavendish Square I came 'ome, I always lived with my aunt and uncle, and I thought I'd stay with 'em and work for 'em, for they'd never throw me out on the streets, I said I'd never work in a fancy house again, too many rules, and they said they'd put money by for me."

"Tell me more about Cavendish Square," Emily said. "Please tell me everything you remember."

But Delia had tired of her London experience and went on to speak of her marriage plans, and Emily's questions about Troy were avoided, because her mind was full of her fiancé. But there were other reasons too – Delia thought that perhaps Troy had tired of his wife, after all, she was plain enough, and never the life and soul of the party – and that he taken her up to the North and abandoned her there – maybe he had injured her and then he had run off. Miss Lucas – or Mrs Troy as she was now – was a nice soul, very innocent, not at all a match for the misfortunes of life or the cunning ways of people. She said so to her Aunt Joan.

"She wor a lady of the 'ouse, a poor relation we know, but not one of us. She was supposed to marry well, but she marries Troy, fell in love with 'im I suppose, an' Troy thought 'e was made up moneywise, for even the poorest of them is richer than us, but and now 'es gone, with all 'er money I suppose, and she's lost 'er memory, and she's as poor now as any beggar, and was in a workhouse. She fell so low! Imagine, I'm the boss of 'er now, and it used to be th'other way round – not that I ever took orders from 'er, she never gave any, she was always unsure of 'erself."

Having heard that she was in London, Emily was not sure if there was anything to be gained now by returning to Bristol.

PUDDING CLUB

Emily was perturbed that there was no reply from Troy. Delia kept her opinions to herself.

The days were getting longer. To her surprise, she was putting up weight.

Delia's aunt took her aside one day. "I think," she said, "that you're in the puddin' club."

"The what?" Emily was completely puzzled. Pudding club! What did it mean?

"When were you last wi' your 'usband?"

"I don't know, I don't remember." She flushed. It was so awful not to be able to remember even her wedding!

"You still don't know what I mean, do you? I think you're going to 'ave a fam'ly."

"A what?" Emily did not understand the dialect.

"A fam'ly, a wean, a baby!"

A baby! Emily was stunned, thrilled, frightened, then all three again. She was like this for the rest of the day and for several days afterwards. She had a persistent thought in her mind – she would have to go to Troy before the child was born!

What was she to do? Her pay was very meagre after board and lodging were deducted from it; she had nothing good to pawn or sell, and she had to save money to get herself to London. The only way was walking or by train, but the train cost a penny a mile, and London was at least one hundred miles away, there were twelve pennies in a shilling, it would be eight shillings and fourpence – well beyond her reach. She would have to feed herself too and eat well for the baby's sake...the stagecoach had long ceased to run, unable to compete with the faster trains. She began to take mending from the lodgers for extra pennies and worked late at night stitching on loose buttons and patching elbows. She could not afford any little luxuries for herself, or go to the fairs or circuses that Delia and her family often went to. Even then, she may have to walk part of the way to London to save money. She even considered going round by water, but it seemed to her that being alone and trapped on a boat with sailors was not to be desired.

One day, she overheard one lodger giving directions to another to find a tavern. "At the end of that street there's a little white chapel, and you turn right there, and the Jolly Roger is a little way up th'hill..."

The words white chapel rang a bell in her mind. "Delia," she said when she was next able to talk to her: "Was there a white chapel anywhere near where we were living? I was wondering if I was married there!"

"No, I never saw one, but – I know! Whitechapel! It's a district of London in the East End. I think Troy was from there – yes, 'e was."

"That's why it seemed familiar," said Emily. "I must go there."

"You need to go to 'im, with baby on th'way. You won't be able to work. He 'as to stand by you even if 'e doesn't want to."

"What do you mean?"

Delia had not meant to speak those words. But they were out now.

"I mean, 'ow did you get up 'ere all th'way from London? Either you ran off or –"

"You think my own husband brought me up here and abandoned me?"

Delia looked flustered.

"I'm sure 'e didn't know you was in the fam'ly way," she said generously.

Emily touched the locket.

"Are you sure this is Troy from Whitechapel and in service in Cavendish Square?"

"I'd swear it on my mother's grave it's 'im."

"And – is Troy his Christian name or his surname?"

"I don't reetly know tha' – we just called 'im Troy."

Delia had left Cavendish square before the mistress had decided to go abroad and she assumed that Mrs Darcy still lived there and that the staff was still intact, and that perhaps Troy still worked there also.

"Are you sure you're married to Troy, Em'ly?"

"Of course I'm sure. Why would I carry around a locket of someone not my husband? I told you, they cut the wedding ring off me."

Aunt Joan gave Emily one sheet of paper and an envelope from the locked cupboard from where they doled them out to sell to the lodgers. She parted with a penny for them and bore them up to her attic together with a pen and a bottle of ink, also from the cupboard.

Dearest Troy, this is Emily. I am in Stockton-on-Tees in the North of England.

She hardly knew what to write to this man who was her husband and a stranger! However, she went on:

Troy, we have so much to talk of. You must have been longing to hear from me by now. I cannot explain anything until I see you. Please come and fetch me to London soon, or send the train fare, if you can.

She hesitated before adding *Your Loving Wife, Emily,* almost feeling like a fraud.

Some days later, the letter arrived at Cavendish Square.

"For Troy, but it just says 'Troy' on the outside." Mr Sallins said, his feet up on the table in the breakfast room. It was sunny there in the mornings. Around them, the furniture was covered in sheets except for the table and two chairs. "That is very odd indeed!"

"A woman's hand," his wife said, pouring coffee out of Mrs Darcy's silver pot and into her best china.

"Postmarked Stockton. Where on earth is that? Oh, it's Durham, up North."

"We shall have to open it and see, for I think the address is most odd. What can she want with him?"

They opened the letter and read it together.

"Astounding! From an Emily who thinks she is the wife of our Troy, who we know to be in Europe with the mistress!"

"What shall we do? Forward it to him?"

"It is very mysterious. What is the address on it?"

"A men's lodging house in Eccles Yard. The paper is cheap and grubby, the pen scratchy."

"Should we look into it further? Should we reply, or forward it?"

"I do not know. Who is Emily?"

It never occurred to them that this 'Emily' was none other than the poor relation of their mistress.

"It's a hoax, for she has not got his full name, but simply 'Troy'. Perhaps a lass who fell in love with him and is suffering the pangs of disappointment."

"We should just throw it away, then."

There was a fire in the room; he crunched it into a ball and threw it into the flames.

After it was done, Mrs Sallins had a dreadful thought.

"It's her! It's Miss Lucas!"

But her husband did not believe her.

"I tell you, it is. I saw them look at each other more than once."

"You are ridiculous, Mrs Sallins. We cannot do anything about it now, in any case."

MR HALLEY'S TROUBLE

Mr Halley was at his club in the City – he had had a bad game of poker and while he was still sober was contemplating his losses. That, with his other debts, made the sale of some of his properties in the North more likely. Not that they mattered much to him – he rarely went there, and he had nobody to leave them to except an undeserving cousin in Barbados. His latest excursion to Durham had been very unpleasant.

He ambled into the comfortable, quiet, leather-outfitted bar. There were men he knew there chatting together, but he was not in the mood for jollity tonight, so he sat at a table with his back to them.

"Whiskey and water," he said to the waiter. "On second thoughts, make it neat, and a double."

"Yes, sir." The waiter sped away.

"Halley! How are you, old man?"

He turned his head, a little irritated. It was Billings, an attorney he knew with whom he had a conversation every now and then, usually of a political nature, for they were both in agreement about the state of the Empire.

"I do all right. And you?"

"Very well, Halley. May I join you for a few minutes?"

Halley made an unenthusiastic sound in the affirmative and Billings took the other chair.

"I have news I thought you might be interested in, Halley."

"What's that?"

"I got a telegraph this morning from Switzerland."

Halley's glass arrived, and a jug of water that the waiter thought wise to put upon the table.

"Switzerland?"

"I am attorney to the widow of George Darcy, name of Lydia. I know you are a friend of hers."

"That my good man, is debatable."

"Oh dear, a falling-out? I was not aware."

Halley said nothing for a moment, and then asked:

"I am still curious about her concerns, however. What was in the telegraph?"

"I brought it with me, in hopes of seeing you here, and I was in luck."

Billings reached into an inner pocket and brought out a folded piece of paper which he smoothed out before handing it to Mr Halley to read. The latter fumbled for his eye glass, leaned toward the light on the table and read it.

MY DEAR BILLINGS I AM ALONE IN SWITZERLAND STOP ROBBED BY MY FOOTMAN HAVE NO MONEY STOP SEND TWO HUNDRED POUNDS STOP

Halley put down his eyeglass and his eyebrows shot up.

"Well well well! What an excellent joke!"

"Is that all you can say? I thought you would be concerned."

Mr Halley put away his monocle.

"Mrs Darcy had an infatuation for this Greek god footman and whisked him off to Europe in hopes of marrying him. I'm not surprised it turned out the way it did. She was an utter fool."

This was news to Mr Billings; astonishment spread over his countenance.

"This footman – was he young, or –?"

"He's a youth, and he must have discovered her real age." Halley said. He took a drink from his glass and laughed heartily. "What a joke!"

"You're not at all concerned then, old chap?"

"About Mrs Darcy? No, for she is well able to look out for herself. And she imposed upon me to allow this –- this cradle-snatching to happen. I did her a favour against my better judgement! Now I see it was all for nothing. He took off with her money! He will hardly return to England –" Halley broke off suddenly, remembering that there was a young Mrs Troy that he might wish to return to. His mood altered. He became quiet, all jollity gone. Mr Billings went on:

"Hardly, if he has any sense. Let us hope, Halley, that the Swiss police catch the young buck and throw him in a jail cell. In the meantime, I had better send some money through the banks. She can live on credit until it arrives, I am sure."

"Let me know if you hear from her again," Halley called after him as he left. He was perturbed by this development. His own crime could be uncovered by young Troy, if he returned to England, and while he could buy and bribe his way out of punishment, he did not like to think of the trouble he would have to go to. As for Troy's thieving, Halley was not sure if he could be prosecuted for a crime committed in another country, but if he did return, Halley could make trouble for him to keep his silence. He was still a wealthy man – money could buy anything.

TROY CONFRONTS HALLEY

Troy had had a smooth journey back to England. He reached his home in Whitechapel on a fresh spring evening and caused great surprise.

"Troy, we're so sorry that Emily went away. If only she had told us where she was going, or told us what 'appened, or if we had offended her in some way, but she went out one Sunday and never came back –"

Troy held up his hand.

"She was kidnapped," he said.

This put the episode into an entirely different light, and his parents felt very guilty indeed that they had doubted her character.

"What do you know about what happened?" he asked them.

"She was seen gettin' into a fine carriage, of 'er own accord too! No wonder we thought she ran off, forgive us, lad."

"Why didn't you write and let me know she was gone?" Troy asked.

"I wrote, I wrote!" his father defended himself. "The letter must have gone astray – the Albert Hotel."

"The Albertine Hotel, it was, Father. There's another hotel some distance away with the name Albert."

"I'm sorry I got that wrong," said Mr Troy. "I should have bin more careful, but these foreign names..."

"How is Mrs Darcy?" his mother was eager for news of the lady.

He took a deep breath and told them the news of the last weeks in Switzerland and how he had found the letter incriminating her.

"She – she did it? She arranged for Emily to be taken away?" They were aghast.

"Yes, with an accomplice who kept Emily at his home for the night in hopes of forcing her to marry him. Thank goodness we had married before I left. He threw her out and she ended up in a workhouse in County Durham and that's all I know."

"A workhouse!" they chorused in horror.

"I'm going North tomorrow to fetch her," he said. "As for the man Halley, I'll 'ave to pay a call on 'im first thing tomorrow morning."

His father took a deep breath and sucked on his pipe.

"I 'ave a question for you, Jimmy, and I'm not tryin' to make difficulties or throw doubts on any part of your story, but why 'asn't Emily written to us 'ere, if she's free?"

He had not thought of that.

"I suppose she isn't as free as I thought," he said. "Maybe they're not allowed to write from workhouses."

There was a silence because his parents did not believe this.

"Many inmates can't write, but she, with 'er education, an' all, she'd 'ave written," his father said slowly. "I never 'eard that inmates couldn't write out."

"I don't know," Troy said. "But I'm going to Durham tomorrow."

They were unhappy to part with him so soon again.

"What are you going to do now, son? You have no job. And I bet no character either. It's not going to be easy."

"I will be orright. I 'ave money I took from Mrs Darcy, it was Emily's money. She was supposed to spend it on 'er and kept it for 'erself."

They were very worried to hear this, because if Mrs Darcy felt she was robbed she could send the police, and as Whitechapel had a bad name the police would believe her. Troy could be ruined and they could never hold up their heads again.

The following morning he was knocking on the door belonging to Mr Halley.

"Mr Halley is not at home," said the aged man with some pomposity.

"Where is he?"

"He is at his seat in the North of England."

"Do I 'ave to send the police to verify 'e's not in this house?"

The ancient man looked horrified.

"The police! Here! Never!"

"I don't wish to be disrespectful to you, sir, but I will send 'em, for I have just cause which I needn't go into here, for I don't rightly know where Mr Halley's seat is exactly, except that it should be on a 'ard bench in the bridewell."

The man wiped a bony hand across his bald head.

"Wait here," he said imperiously. He went upstairs and returned five minutes later.

"Come in."

Troy waited in the same musty drawing room that Mrs Darcy had been in plotting against Emily. The door creaked open and Mr Halley stepped in in his dressing gown.

"Troy," he said smoothly. They knew each other from a few at-homes at Cavendish Square. Halley was known to Troy as the man who always wanted more and stronger spirits than anybody else; Troy had caught Halley's attention because of his bearing and good looks, and Lydia's love for him had not really been a surprise.

"Where's my wife?"

Halley went to the sideboard and poured himself a double shot of whiskey. "Would you like one?"

"No," said Troy shortly. "Where's my wife?" His voice was raised. "I know what happened – she was taken to your place in Durham, and is now in a workhouse, and I want to know which one."

"My place as you call it is about thirty miles north of Stockton-on-Tees," he said, "and the last I heard she is in the workhouse about two miles away, down the hill toward the village of Grimton. You surprise me, Troy-boy. You had a chance to better yourself, and become a gentleman like me, and you threw it all away for the poor relation. Of course, she raises you up a notch or two, but you could have risen much further. How is Mrs Darcy?"

"I have no idea how she is," Troy said. "Nor do I care."

"Don't burn all your bridges," Halley's next words were. "Your wife won't know you. She had an accident (which was nothing to do with me) and lost her memory. You see, your remark about the police did not frighten me at all. She has no memory of how she came to be up North. She's forgotten you also, and only that they had to cut the ring away from her finger, nobody would know she was married. You could safely leave her there and nobody would be any the wiser. Mrs Darcy will forgive you and take you back, she is in love with you, very much in love."

"Forgive me what?" Troy was suspicious.

"For leaving her and – you know. Theft."

Troy did not care to hear any more. So Mrs Darcy had got a message to Halley. Perhaps she hated him now with as much passion as she had loved him, for on the long hours on the trains and boat, Troy had gone over everything in his mind, and what he had seen clearly was her single-minded determination to have him. To own him. To have ruined Emily's life in order to have her heart's desire!

"So if I were you, I would forget the woman you married in haste and call your wife, and return to Lydia Darcy. She, as her guardian, could claim that the girl did not ask her consent, and the whole thing could be annulled with the help of a clever ecclesiastical lawyer."

Troy had no answer for this, except to call Halley a few names not to be repeated here.

"I was trying to give you a warning, nicely," said Halley, finishing his glass. "It would be a shame to get the police involved."

"For you, sir. Not for me. What I took from Mrs Darcy was mine in fact. It was belonging to my wife. The envelope even has her name upon it; yes, I still have the envelope. Mrs Darcy had no claim on it."

"Get out."

"Gladly, sir."

He made an exit and banged the door hard.

He left Mr Halley in a state of some worry.

She will remember me, Troy thought, she will. When she sees me, she will remember me!

Troy's next stop was to Cavendish Square, where he found Mr and Mrs Sallins curating the empty home and far too curious about why he had returned alone. He told them that he was not in Mrs Darcy's employ anymore, and that if they were to hear from Miss Emily Lucas who was now his wife that they were to contact him at Whitechapel without delay.

"You married Miss Lucas!"

"Yes, why are you surprised? Did you not wonder where I went when I got up from the table in the servant's hall early, leaving you to your gossip? Could you not tell why I couldn't bear any gossip about 'er?"

"That was very bad of you, not to tell me," exploded Mr Sallins. The couple looked at each other, guilt and confusion overcoming them.

"The talk at the table was something awful," Troy said evenly.

"And here we were, thinking you were married now to the mistress." Mrs Sallins said in a very rapid way. "Or perhaps in the fashion of rich women marrying inferior men, you would have become Mr Darcy, but I hope you didn't leave the mistress with a broken heart, that would be caddish, after all, you paid her every attention, and –"

Mr Sallins interrupted.

"—it is most odd that you came back here, and say that you have left her for good, when she could have given you a great future, how ungrateful of you, an age difference is not significant, I'm sure she would have made you a splendid wife, and..."

It seemed to Troy that they were talking too quickly and fidgeting and not meeting his eye.

"I never paid 'er attention beyond what was due a servant to an employer, what rubbish! You know something I don't know, what is it?" he wished to know, and they confessed to him that they had received a letter from 'Emily' but not understanding it, had thrown it in the fire.

"So you do not have any address for her?"

They shook their heads.

"Please, please try to remember!"

"Barnes, Barnes Lodging, maybe."

"Barnes?" Troy frowned, then looked at Mrs Sallins. "Wasn't that Delia's surname? Remember Delia, who worked here? Was she not from Stockton-on-Tees?"

"Why yes she was!"

They hurried to the housekeeper's rooms, and Mrs Sallins opened her bureau and looked among the many applications she had there for servant positions. And at last she found it - Bedelia Barnes, 4 Eccles Yard. Stockton-on-Tees.

TURTLEDOVES

He took the next train to Stockton-on-Tees. It was a long journey. As he went north it seemed to him that he was entering a wild, deserted country. It had beauty but a harshness also, as if used to wild weather. Thousands of sheep made snowy patches in the rugged fields as the train chugged along. Cattle with long hairy coats stared at them as they went past, as if they could see through the long hair covering their eyes. Walls were made of rocks, and high stone houses with narrow windows built to withstand gales. Stony sheds in the middle of the fields. And then they were approaching Stockton – railroad tracks, more houses, warehouses, factories – the train screeched to a halt at the station, already distinguished in the realm of railroad history. In 1825 the first passenger steam train in the world left from Stockton in a short trip to nearby Darlington, ushering in a new age of travel. But Troy was in too much of a hurry to read the plaque proclaiming the station's impressive history and hurried past it to find his wife.

Fifteen minutes later he was in Eccles Yard and at the boarding house, entering by the lodger's door which led into their eating area. The lodgers were still out at work and the girls were setting the tables.

"Well if it isn't Troy!" said an amazed Delia, who saw him first. "Troy from London!"

"Hallo Delia! It's me orright. Where's my Emily? Is she 'ere?"

He had not noticed the drab-clothed woman in the shadows with her back to him. She turned around, his eyes lit up – it was his beloved Emily.

As she came toward him Emily's heart did a somersault – here was the man from the portrait, here was her husband, and that was all she knew of him except that he was a footman in London. Her eyes looked to him quizzically.

He took her hands in his.

"I heard you lost your memory, turtledove. Is it true? Do you not know me?" He sounded pained. Emily did not like strangers. Was he a stranger to her? Would they have to begin all over again?

"Turtledove," she repeated softly, as if wondering. "My heart knows you, even if my head has trouble catching up with it." He smiled in relief and gently tried to draw her closer.

She tapped the locket around her neck and opened it.

He brought its counterpart from under his collar and snapped it open.

"See? There's your portrait."

She seemed really pleased, and her eyes shining at last, embraced him.

"Has your memory come back, then, that you knew where to find me?" he asked her.

"Not really," Emily whispered. "Had it not been for Bedelia, I would not have known where you were."

"Are you still in service there, then?" Delia asked, moving closer, a bit jealous of the two lovebirds, still thinking that Troy was wasted on Emily Lucas. "Is Chalamet still there, and the others?"

He looked from one to the other.

"Oh no," he said. "You don't know – how am I going to piece it all together to tell you? Can I sit down? Can I get a cup o' tea?"

ALL HOPE GONE

Lydia Darcy spent her days angry, embittered, and vowing revenge on her cousin and Troy. The betrayal from him hurt her deeply, not that she had ever asked anything of him, but his desertion felt like betrayal.

The short, terse note replayed itself in her head over and over. He did not have to write at length to express how little in esteem he held her. The contempt shouted itself from the few words. He cared nothing for her.

Worst of all, he loved Emily. He loved Emily, that shy, dowdy country girl. It was infuriating. A man like Troy was thoroughly wasted on Emily Lucas. She would never bring him anything of value in life.

Unable to bear the common people she was forced to board with, she sold some jewellery in order to move into another expensive hotel. She would wait there until the money arrived from England but what should she do then? Her London house did not attract her, and she did not know where she would settle or what she would do with herself in the future.

She was lonely and felt abandoned and sought to catch the eyes of the unaccompanied young gentlemen, but without Chalamet's particular skill she knew that she either looked almost forty or that she appeared caked in creams or powders. Neither look was attractive to the young gentlemen on their world tours, so she lingered alone at her meals, sighing to herself and wondering if she was going to be alone for the rest of her life.

She was at lunch one day when the concierge walked in with a telegram on a tray. "For you, Madame. I'm afraid it arrived at the Albertine late last night, and it took the post office all morning to find you here."

A telegram! Her first thought was that it must be Troy – Troy, repentant, begging! She would take him back in an instant!

She opened it with detachment.

DAPHNE MORTALLY ILL STOP COME QUICKLY STOP HEADMISTRESS WINTERLEA SCHOOL

She did not understand it –

Daphne was so little in her mind that for a moment she wondered why she of all people should get a telegraph if her daughter was mortally ill.

Then the dining room seemed to fade away – the voices of the other diners became murmurs, the room darkened and she saw only herself. She seemed to be in front of herself, looking at herself as in a mirror, she saw herself seated at the table, moving and reading the telegram and frowning. Then her body faded and she beheld a shape within her that should have been glowing and beautiful, but it was not. She knew that this was her soul, and it was a dreadful sight. There were holes of rotteness and decay. She cried out in terror.

"Madam, it is bad news?" She was back in her own body, the vision over, and she fell insensible to the floor. The other diners came to her assistance.

A few hours later she, with the urgent assistance of the Hotel, was waiting in the train station, her bags in the porter's office waiting to be put on the First Class Luggage car. She walked up and down the platform not really seeing anybody. She wandered up to the bridge over the railway lines by which one could cross to the other platform. She stayed on the bridge, looking out on the lines below, her gloved hand on the railing, and she began to feel great bitterness.

Her thoughts about herself were so dreadful that she could not stand them. Her daughter could be dead by the time she got to England, and she had never known her, never loved her, never cherished her. She was a horrible mother. She heard the pleas in Daphne's letters – she wanted a mother's love so much, and Lydia had set the letters aside, too intent on pursuing her own desires to give any heed to them.

God, she was sure, was very angry with her. He had stormed off and given her up for good.

She heard a whistle and up the line she espied a train about to come to the station – it was not slowing down, and she guessed that it would go swiftly through. A thought came to her. A temptation – as she watched the smoke come nearer, she thought she would end her own life. She would throw herself on the tracks in the train's path. Who would care? Who would miss her? She began to lean over.

Her movements attracted the attention of the guard on the platform, who guessing her intent, shouted a warning to the people on the bridge, and two women near her immediately saw what was about to take place. They ran, one to each side of her and secured her. She fought them, but they were too strong for her, and the train passed underneath, and she burst into tears of anger and despair.

They happened to be two nursing nuns from the hospital.

She was led to the platform again. Why were these people involved with her? They could not know her, if they knew her, they would go from her in disgust and leave her to her own punishment.

"Leave me alone, I am in despair," she wept. "There is no hope!"

"You are ill, Madame. What is the matter?"

She told them that her daughter may be dead in England, and that she would not reach her in time to say goodbye. There was no need to pour out her soul to them. They persuaded her to continue her journey to England, but two of the nuns were sent to accompany her to make sure she did not attempt to hurt herself again. Lydia did not object. A passivity had overcome her. Let the nuns do as they wished with her, she did not care. She was led to the station, her bags were put on board the train, she was led to a seat, she was told to eat so she ate, she was told to drink so she drank, she was told to sleep and she slept. She felt utterly numb for the first day of travel, but then, she began to talk. The women listened as she poured out her heart and bared the state of her soul, though she did not think it proper to tell them that she loved chasing young men, so she left that out. She told them that she was selfish, always pursuing her own pleasures, and had neglected her little daughter. And she had been most unkind to a poor cousin who had been sent to her to care for. She didn't know where that girl was now.

"My soul must be lost," she said simply. "God could not possibly like me."

"You must not believe you are lost," Sister Francine said to her. "He will save you. He loves to heal and save souls from despair and sin. And we will pray for Daphne." And so their conversations went every day, as the trains hurtled past towns and fields of men ploughing and sowing their crops.

And so Lydia began to see that her old life must go, she must leave it behind her as she was leaving Switzerland and France and the prospect of marriage to Troy. By the time they reached Calais, she felt a great deal stronger in her soul and mind. She had left despair behind and her one focus now – to be a good mother to Daphne, if God spared her daughter's life!

She said goodbye to Sisters Francine and Louise. Lydia obtained their address so that they could correspond.

"Remember to pray," said Sister Francine, holding both of her hands in hers before they parted. "And we will pray for you." They had given her the words to a hymn that had been written some years before. It had been written by a great sinner, they explained, before he found God. He had been involved in the Slave Trade, and had been shipwrecked. He had repented. His name was John Newton, and he wrote *Amazing Grace, how sweet the sound, that saved a wretch like me. I once was lost, but now I'm found, was blind but now I see.'* These words found a home with Lydia Darcy. They seemed to describe her. There were other souls like her, then? She repeated them to herself on the ship and on the train as it hurtled toward Oxfordshire where Daphne was.

She arrived at the school at ten o'clock at night and the persistent knocking woke the Headmistress, who let her in. "She is still with us!" The words were music to Lydia's ears as Miss Carruthers hurried her along passage after passage by candlelight. At last they reached the quiet, dark infirmary. A few hushed words to the nurse at the desk, and she was led to a bed in the corner, the only sounds being the quiet breathing of the several little patients they passed.

"Here she is," whispered the nurse, holding the lantern close to the pillow.

Lydia looked down upon the little face so like her own, her eyes closed in sleep. One of her hands was outside the covers laying on the sheet. She took it.

"My poor child!" she said, unable to check the tears any longer, tears of relief and gratitude, holding the little hand to her cheek.

The eyes opened. "Mamma! Is it really you?"

Lydia gathered the child in her arms and wept.

"Don't cry, Mamma," Daphne's muffled voice rose from somewhere in the furs covering her mother's bosom, "I'm going to be all right. The doctor said so yesterday." She raised her head and turned to the nurse. "Didn't he, Nurse Barton, didn't the doctor say I was going to be all right?"

"He did, that he did," said the nurse warmly.

"So you see, Mamma, there's no need at all to cry!" Daphne wiped her mother's tears away with her fingers.

BACK TO CAVENDISH SQUARE

"Don't cry, turtledove, your memory will come back, and maybe it's just as well you don't remember our wedding, cos it was a very plain, rushed affair, and no frills or flounces, or guests, no photograph as everybody wants now, and then I 'ad to go back to work, and you went to my parents and we were together that night – the night afore I left for the continent." He touched her stomach tenderly. "We 'ad a lovely night an' God blessed us, din't He. Then I 'ad to go back to the House an' get ready for the sailing. Now don't cry. That madman in the North din't touch you. I 'ave it 'ere in this letter, you met in the morning, and then 'e threw you out. What if you and I take a little journey up there to find out more? If you don't want to, that is orright. I 'ave money for you. It's enough to set up house you an' me. We'll be 'appy in our little nest, and Baby makes three."

She threw her arms about his neck and clung to him.

"Everything is coming back to me slowly," she said. "But I'd rather go to London and then we'll go over all the places I was supposed to have been, I'm sure the Sallinses at Cavendish will let us visit."

"You were a member of the family there, they can't keep you out. Whatever about me. And we'll stay for a while with my Ma and Pa in Whitechapel. It's a lovely little 'ouse, though Whitechapel itself isn't much."

She took leave of the Barnes family and the lodging house. They had been good to her when she had needed it, though she had no idea that they had gotten a cook so cheaply. She and Troy departed on the London train for the long journey away from the sheep and moors to the south.

"You have my money? I'm so glad you got it back," she said. "And I'd rather spend it setting up house for Baby than on crinolines and fans."

Troy did not want to worry her about Halley's threat. He wondered what Mrs Darcy's intentions were. Would she try to avenge herself?

They went straight to Whitechapel. His parents were not expecting them as he had not had time to write them; however they rallied quickly from the surprise and embraced Emily and tried to make her comfortable, though she did not remember them at all and looked lost and crestfallen. She was very tired and she and Troy retired early to bed.

"I hope it's our grandchild she's carryin'," Mrs Troy said, putting the dishes back on the dresser. "It could be that horrible fellow up North that abducted 'er."

"We just have to trust it's our grandchild, luv. The poor woman's been through an ordeal, and had a horrible accident into the bargain, we should go out of our way to be good to 'er, we've already misjudged 'er."

His wife said nothing.

"Look luv, you've not lost Troy. You've gained a daughter. There."

His wife poked the fire.

"I know," she said. "I just find it 'ard to get used to new relations, you're supposed to love 'em without knowing 'em. And he's our only, and that makes it worse."

"And she probably feels the same way. We 'ave to make the effort."

"I will, Charlie. But I'm still worried the police will come 'ere."

"Stop worryin'. You see our Troy. He's an honest man. Nothing will 'appen."

The following day Emily seemed more at ease with them. She had found her clothes in the room and she recognised them and remembered even when she had purchased the materials and the hats and gloves. She brightened.

A few days later the young couple set out for Cavendish Square. They found the house buzzing, quite a change from when Troy had visited on the last occasion. They found the butler and housekeeper bustling about the hallway supervising a bevy of servants.

Sallins reported that the servants had been called back; they were re-opening the house for the mistress was returning – with her child.

"Mrs Troy, I believe," Sallins bowed to Emily. But there was little respect in his address, he exuded flippancy, even contempt. His wife was more enthused.

"I never knew this was going on under my nose! I should scold you, you bad girl!"

"Miss Lucas was not a servant, Mrs Sallins." Troy said. "Her business was none of your business."

"But your business was my business," Sallins cut in.

"I'll take a look around the house," Emily said, making for the stairs. "Which was my room?"

Troy was able to tell her that, and Mr Sallins could not stop them from going up and looking about the rooms upstairs.

"Here's where we used to meet," Troy said, when they came to the bottom of the servant's stairs. "Oh you do remember, don't you? I can see you do!"

"Persia the chaperone cat! Remember her staring us down!" giggled Emily.

They embraced again in a long kiss.

"We're in need of a footman, if yer interested!" Sallins said in a sarcastic way to Troy as they came back down.

"No thank you!" Troy retorted back.

"I suppose she will want a handsome young man again," said Mrs Sallins in a throwaway manner.

The Troy's let themselves out the front door.

"I don't want to meet that woman when she comes back," Troy said.

"I do," Emily said suddenly.

"You'll 'ave to do so on your own, then. I can't stand the sight of 'er after what she did."

"I want to see her. I remember bits and pieces of my weeks here, Troy. The hall, the back garden, the dog! How lovely it was that he rushed out to meet me!"

Oswald, the spaniel, had thrown himself upon Emily when she had stepped into the back garden. He had caused a flood of little pieces of memory to return, like pieces of a jigsaw. She had beamed from ear to ear as he jumped into her arms and licked her face all over.

MEETING LYDIA AGAIN

Emily paid her a call one morning soon after. She was shown into the drawing room, the same room where she had stood, awkward and unhappy only a year before, but she did not remember that, and looked about to see if anything was familiar, and wondered if she would recognise her cousin.

It was a few minutes before Cousin Lydia appeared. She came into the room rather quietly, and if Emily's memory had been intact, she would have noted that the arrogant sweep that had marked her entrances before was absent. There was another difference she would have seen also. She had lines and wrinkles and looked years older – there were no cosmetics.

"Cousin Lydia?" Emily said.

"Cousin Emily," said Lydia.

They sat down on opposite sides of the fire screen. It was too warm for a fire.

"I wanted to see you." Emily said.

Lydia nodded vaguely.

"I'm afraid I don't remember you," Emily said then. "I remember rooms and places and streets, but so far, not people. I hope you don't mind."

"I do not mind. I am rather happy you do not remember me. I wish you never would remember me. I am ashamed of what I have been. It was before."

"Before?"

"Before I saw myself, my soul. It's too complicated to go into. Did you know my child became very ill?"

"A child?"

"Yes, I have a daughter. You have never met her, in case you're wondering if you should remember her too."

"Is she recovered?"

"Yes, almost fully recovered. We'll spend a few weeks here, just enough time for me to quit this house for good and then we'll go to Oxfordshire, near to her school and to her friends the Alcotts, who are almost family to my little girl. She misses them. She is my life now. I almost lost her."

Mrs Darcy paused. After the initial rapture of meeting her mother, little Daphne had begun to miss the Alcotts. She had even told her mother that Mrs Alcott was better at curling her hair than she was. This had hurt Lydia, but she reflected that she deserved it – 'you reap what you sow,' she had said to herself. Building the mother-daughter bond would take time and patience.

"Will you forgive me all I've done?" Mrs Darcy said then.

"I don't really remember what you've done," Emily said truthfully. "Others have told me, but I don't remember. I don't even remember my wedding. I suppose I ought to ask your forgiveness too for that, as I was under your care."

"I was bad at caring. You have cause to have me jailed."

"Of course you know I'm not going to do that."

"It is good to know."

"Troy sends his regards." Emily got up to go. Mrs Darcy nodded. "Oh, wait – I would so like you to meet Daphne. Would you – will you meet her?"

"Of course!"

A few moments later a young girl bounced into the room, all smiles. She went straight to her mother's side and put her arms about her. Her mother's arms encircled her.

"This is Cousin Emily," said her mother to her. The girl's eyes were smiling as she curtsied. For a fleeting moment Emily remembered her own mother – her dear, loving

Mamma. The love between a mother and child was unique and irreplaceable if lost.

No matter what she's done, she thought to herself of Lydia, she has seen herself and is trying to be better. I wish them well. I wish that Troy would stop being so bitter on my behalf.

BECOMING DAPHANE'S MOTHER

Mrs Lydia Darcy had one more task before she left London for good. Leaving Daphne with her governess one day, she again took the carriage to Mr Halley's home. As with Troy, he was 'not at home' but she stood her ground, convincing the butler that it was very important.

"I am here to say I am sorry," she told Mr Halley when he appeared, bloated and purple-faced after a night's drinking. They sat in his cheerless room after he had poured himself a glass of brandy.

"You've changed," was his response. "No more paint, eh? What are you sorry for in particular? My part in abducting Miss Lucas, or the threat to spread that lie about the boy in Bangalore?"

She lowered her eyes to the frayed and dull carpet.

"I'm sorry for everything. Yes, I knew it was a lie, my husband believed it to be a lie. It was not you who injured the lad."

"Once a person's character is tainted with association, there is no redress, no rehabilitation, because people will always wonder."

She looked her sorrow rather than repeated it.

"And what is so new with you that you've abandoned all pretentions to youth?" He spoke bitterly.

She told him about her experience in Switzerland upon receipt of the telegram that her child was ill.

"It was a great grace given to me by God to see my soul thus."

"I wonder what mine's like, worse I'm sure."

Lydia brought out a card from her pocket.

"Please take this and read it," she said. "It was given to me by two nuns abroad. It has been my lifeline."

"There's no hope for someone like me," he said, waving it away.

"I thought that about myself," she said. "I was wrong. It is still hard, though. I still want to think of Troy, to dream of him, but I must turn quietly away from that, for I made an idol of him. I know that now."

"Your life can't be much fun now."

"I have my daughter. Don't you have anybody to care for, Halley?"

He looked at his glass, swirling the amber liquid about in it.

"I have a cousin in the United States," he said. "He is my heir, and wealthy in his own right. I do not know him. On the other hand, I have injured many people. If I were to reform my life, I would try to make good there."

"Go and see your priest," Mrs Darcy urged, "for you cannot do it alone. You need a different set of friends also. Begin again, George! Stay in touch with me, and we can encourage each other."

Mrs Darcy rose to go. She left the card with 'Amazing Grace' on the table. It would be up to Mr Halley to attempt a turn-about in his life. Nobody can decide that but the person themselves.

LIVING LIFE AND RAISING A FAMILY

"I'm quite fond of Emily now," Nell Troy said to her husband one evening when their grandson was a year old and delighted his grandparents from one end of the day to the other. "She's quiet and not a gossip; I know everything that passes 'ere will not go past those doors. I trust 'er. She took a long time to get to know, though. I'm glad our Troy married 'er. She's a nice girl and is a loving mother to young Charles Lucas Troy. I'll miss 'em when they get their own house."

Another baby was born two years later, a little girl named Mary Ellen. By then, the young family had moved to outside London, to Sussex, to a newly-built modest cottage near the new Lord Edward Hotel, where Troy worked as Head Porter.

The only communication from Mrs Darcy was a 'character' or a glowing reference written in a professional manner for Troy sent by post from her new home in Oxfordshire. She and Troy never met again, and Troy found his way to forgiveness also, for Emily in her gentle way reminded him to take seriously the words about 'striving for the Kingdom of God', and bearing grudges was not of God.

When Emily turned twenty-five a surprise awaited her in the form of a letter from her late great-aunt's attorney Mr Weatherstone, informing her that she had been very difficult to find, and would she please give direction as to which Bank he was to direct her inheritance of two thousand pounds?

It was a fortune to the young family. They were able to provide well for Troy's parents, who were humbled by Emily's generous heart. They moved to a larger house so that the old couple could come and live with them. By now Emily was at ease with her in-laws and they with her, and when they were all gathered around a warm fire drinking cocoa on a winter's evening she felt very content – and grateful – to have a family of three generations. She never knew of her mother's last heartfelt prayer, and she did not know that her mother's last prayer had been answered in God's own way and time.

Emily's memories never fully returned from her sojourn in London, but events since were firmly planted and remembered. Her cousin's harshness to her had been erased, and she was glad she did not suffer from the remembrance of it.

Troy was promoted to Junior Manager, and in time, Manager, and was known locally as an upstanding, fair man who had a good word for everybody. He discouraged gossiping in his establishment.

Emily never intended to go and see her mother's people the Lucas' in Devonshire. Their address was long lost and she was not even sure in which village they lived. But one day she discovered that a scullery maid named Tilly Lucas in the hotel could be a young cousin. The girl was miserably homesick and frightened and Emily took her under her wing, and she thrived and was happier. After that, Emily looked out for the homesick and the unhappy in her own home and in the hotel, and she became known as a kind mistress and benefactor, though she never lost her tendency to be reserved. She still had a tendency to dislike strangers but learned that everybody had a fragility in some way and she tried to think the best of everyone. For her, the Gospel commandment to love your neighbour was challenging if she did not know her neighbours, so she set out to do so.

Troy saw in the newspaper that Emily's father had died in Malta, leaving a wife and six children. 'Seven' he muttered to himself, smarting over the neglect of his first child. Emily was sad to hear the news, but she had never known him, and Charlie Troy was her father now.

As she grew older, Emily often reflected on the people she had known throughout her early life.

She resolved to go back to Bristol one summer and take her children also. She visited Yellowhill, and found out where Maria had gone into service. She had married a coachman and they had five living children. Maria remembered the frightened little girl named Emily Lucas. They corresponded until Maria died at the age of seventy.

By now Emily also wanted to go into Devonshire and see the Lucas'. With information from her maidservant from there, she found the village. But her step-brothers and step-sisters had no interest in meeting her, not even Harry who was now headmaster of the little school. Her mother had brought disgrace upon them and they were still stuck at that place. She washed her hands of them for good. The only relation who welcomed her was Tilly's mother.

Michael in Bristol was long dead as was Mrs Anderson. The unflappable Sarah had retired to a home she shared with her widowed sister. And Miss Browne – she managed to find Miss Browne, who told her that she had never liked any place as much as Mrs Loft's after she had left. She was still employed as a governess but planned to retire to a little cottage she had saved all her life to buy.

The Troy's never saw Mr Halley again. He removed himself from London. He paid all his debts and tried to right the wrongs he had done to people. He was never able to forego alcohol until a few weeks before he died. Some of his servants remarked that it was abstinence that killed him and if he had not given it up he'd have lived to a ripe old age. The old butler went to live with his sisters.

They had no contact with Cousin Lydia, but the newspaper carried the notice of Miss Daphne Darcy's marriage to Mr Ashton Venables, which astonished them, and the couple were about to set out for their new home in America after the wedding. There was a story there that Emily would have loved to have known, but some things have to remain unknown.

Troy and Emily lived to see their grandchildren grow up and marry. They lived to see motorcars and telephones. Their favourite invention was the gramophone. Their grandson bought a His Master's Voice gramophone for them before he left for the Great War and their granddaughter gave them a record of Strauss waltzes. They danced the waltz more times than they could count during their long marriage, at hotel dances and functions, and later in their own parlour, but the first enchanting dance in Cavendish Square never left Troy's memory, and he often recounted it to his wife so that in the end, she was convinced that she remembered it as well.

THANK YOU FOR CHOOSING A PUREREAD BOOK!

We hope you enjoyed the story, and as a way to thank you for choosing PureRead we'd like to send you this free book, and other fun reader rewards...

Click here for your free copy of Whitechapel Waif
PureRead.com/victorian

Thanks again for reading.
See you soon!

LOVE VICTORIAN ROMANCE?

If you enjoyed this story why not continue straight away with other books in our PureRead Victorian Romance library?

Read them all...

Victorian Slum Girl's Dream

Poor Girl's Hope

The Lost Orphan of Cheapside

Born a Workhouse Baby

The Lowly Maid's Triumph

Poor Girl's Hope

The Victorian Millhouse Sisters

Dora's Workhouse Child

Saltwick River Orphan

Workhouse Girl and The Veiled Lady

OUR GIFT TO YOU

AS A WAY TO SAY THANK YOU WE WOULD LOVE TO SEND YOU THIS BEAUTIFUL STORY FREE OF CHARGE.

Click here for your free copy of Whitechapel Waif

PureRead.com/victorian

At PureRead we publish books you can trust. Great tales without smut or swearing, but with all of the mystery and romance you expect from a great story.

Be the first to know when we release new books, take part in our fun competitions, and get surprise free books in your inbox by signing up to our free VIP Reader list.

As a welcome gift you'll receive the story of the Whitechapel Waif straight to your inbox...

Click here for your free copy of Whitechapel Waif

PureRead.com/victorian

Printed in Great Britain
by Amazon

40926398R00189